*Mercier Press is the oldest independent Irish
publishing house and has published books in the
fields of history, literature, folklore, music, art,
humour, drama, politics, current affairs, law
and religion. It was founded in 1944 by John
and Mary Feehan.*

*In the building up of a country
few needs are as great as that of a publishing
house which would make the people proud of
their past, and proud of themselves as a people
capable of inspiring and supporting a world of
books which was their very own. Mercier Press
has tried to be that publishing house. On the
occasion of our fiftieth anniversary we thank
the many writers and readers who have
supported us and contributed to our success.*

*We face our second half-century
with confidence.*

More Stories from the Great Irish Writers

SELECTED AND EDITED BY

JOHN McCARTHY

MERCIER PRESS

Mercier Press
PO Box 5, 5 French Church Street, Cork, Ireland

and
24 Lower Abbey Street, Dublin 1, Ireland

© John McCarthy, 1968, 1993, 1994

ISBN 1 85635 085 1

The stories in this book were originally published in the United
States of America as part of *Irish Humor: The Book for All Seasons*
(The Continuum Publishing Company).

Acknowledgements for permission to reprint stories in this
collection can be found on page 160.

More Stories from the Great Irish Writers is published by arrangement
with the Continuum Publishing Company.

First published 1994
10 9 8 7 6 5 4 3 2 1

A CIP catalogue record for this book
is available from the British Library.

Printed in Ireland by Colour Books Ltd.

Contents

Introduction

There are so many good Irish writers that to designate some as great may distress readers who would make a different choice. Tastes differ just as much in books as they do in foods.

There is, however, something which might be termed 'universal appeal'. People the world over are pretty much the same and go through the same cycles. They get born, grow up, have children, establish a home and eventually die.

The Irish are great storytellers – they are also great nomads. They can make themselves at home anywhere. The stories they tell show this deep understanding of human nature – the world at large.

The stories in this collection emphasise that understanding. The ability to survive a bad turn of events with a smile, maybe even a laugh.

They are not stage Irish. They are short stories, beautifully written, portraying the lighter side of life in Ireland or, for that matter, life anywhere.

JOHN MCCARTHY

'ALL THE SWEET BUTTERMILK...'

by Donagh MacDonagh

THE MOST LONESOME PLACE I was ever posted to was a little town twenty miles from the nearest railway, in the County Mayo, where there was neither cinema, theatre nor anything else; the only entertainment was a chat and a smoke, a drink and an occasional dance. I was always a great one to fish and take life easy, so it suited me fine, but the sergeant didn't fancy it at all.

Sergeant Finnegan was a dour-looking man and very close. I never rightly discovered what it was had him shifted to that place, but it can't have been want of zeal. He was the most energetic man and the most enthusiastic man in his search for crime that ever I met. Of course he was wasting his time looking for crime in Coolnamara, but what he couldn't find he invented.

Hanlon and Flaherty and myself used to have a grand easy life of it in old Sergeant Moloney's time; there wasn't a bicycle lamp in the district, the pubs closed when the last customer went home, and that was earlier than you'd think, and if there was any poitín made, nobody came worrying us about it. But Sergeant Finnegan soon changed all that. He wasn't a month in the place till every lad in the county had a lamp on his bike, I even bought one myself; and there was such a row kicked up about the pubs staying open that nobody went home till midnight. They suddenly realised that there must be a great charm in after-hours drinking.

The sergeant used to have me cross-eyed chasing round the county in search of illicit stills, and as soon as ever I'd get settled down for the evening with my pipe going nicely and the wireless behind my head, he'd be in with some new list of outrages, cattle straying on the road, a camp of tinkers that whipped a couple of chickens, or some nonsense like that.

'Take your feet down off that mantelpiece,' he'd say, 'and get down on patrol. Who knows what malicious damage or burglary or larceny is going on under the cover of night!' And up I'd have to get, put on my coat and go in next door to listen to the news.

He was a great man for objecting to dance-hall licences, and if he'd had his way there wouldn't have been a foot put on the floor within the four walls of Ireland. On the night of a dance he'd be snooping around to see was there any infringement of the regulations, and his finger itching on the pencil to make notes for a prosecution.

One night there was an all-night dance over in Ballyduv and he sent me over to keep an eye on it.

'I think I'd better go in mufti, Sergeant,' says I. 'There's no use in drawing their attention to the civic guards being present.'

'True. True. Quite true!' says he. So up I went and changed, chuckling to myself. I could have worn a beard and a major-general's outfit and every hog, dog and devil in the place would have known me. But I always enjoyed a dance and I didn't want to be encumbered with a uniform for the stretch of the evening.

When I got to the dance-hall, it was about half ten but hardly anyone had arrived yet. At an all-night dance they're never in much of a hurry to get started, and besides, the lads have to get washed and changed after the day's work. I stood chatting to Callaghan, that owned the hall, for a bit, and then we went over to Hennessy's for a couple of pints. Of course it was well after hours by this time, but with the sergeant safe in Coolnamara nobody was worrying too much about that. Around about half eleven we heard the band getting into its stride, so we came back to see how the fun was going.

As soon as I stepped in through the door I saw the grandest looking girl you'd want to see, bronze-coloured hair, green eyes, and an American dress that was made for her figure.

'Who's that?' says I to Callaghan. 'She must be down from Dublin.'

'Dublin nothing!' says he. 'She's from the mountain beyond. There's a whole family of them, and they're as wild as a lot of mountain goats. Lynch's they are.'

'Give us a knock-down,' says I. 'I'll surely die if I don't meet that one!'

'I will,' says he, 'but I better say nothing about you being in the guards.'

'And why not?'

'Now never mind. It's what I'm telling you.' So he brought me over and introduced me to her.

Well, we got on grand. There was a waltz just starting and I asked her out, and we danced from that out without a break, and when we were tired dancing we went out for a bit of a walk, and I can tell you I wasn't wasting my time.

She told me all about the sister in America and how anxious she was to get to Dublin, and I could see she was dying down dead to find out who I was, but after Jack Callaghan's warning, I made her no wiser.

On about one o'clock we were whirling around when what should I see sloping through the door but the sergeant, and he in mufti, too. He gave me a very cold nod and I didn't pretend to take the least bit of notice of him.

'Who's your friend?' says she. 'I never saw him before.'

'Any more than you saw me!' says I, giving her a squeeze and avoiding the question.

'Who is he, though?' she said again, so I saw there was no way out of it.

'That's Sergeant Finnegan from Coolnamara,' says I, 'and a greater troublemaker there isn't in the country.'

'And what else would he be only a troublemaker, if he's a

garda. If there's one thing I hate in this world it's a garda, and if there's a thing I hate more it's a sergeant.' I could see I was on very delicate ground and took all the trouble I could not to be any way awkward with my big feet.

'And why is that?' says I, but she only tossed her head and shot the sergeant dead with both her green eyes.

After a bit, some great gawk of a countryman managed to prise her away from me, and off she went, though I felt she'd rather stay.

No sooner had she gone than I could feel the sergeant breathing down the back of my neck.

'Come outside here till I talk to you,' says he, and I could see she had her eyes buried in us as we went out the door.

'Do you know what that is?' says he.

'That's a girl called Maeve Lynch,' says I. 'Isn't she a grand-looking thing?'

'Her father's the greatest poitín maker in the county of Mayo, and I thought you were long enough in the county to know that.'

'Well, that's news to me. He was never prosecuted in my time. How do you know?'

'From information received. Now you keep away from that girl, or it might be worse for you. And keep your mind on your business. Don't you know you have no right to be dancing?'

'I was just seeing could I pick up any information. But things are very quiet.'

'Things are never as quiet as they appear. I hope you investigated Hennessy's after closing time.'

'You can be bound I did!' says I without a smile.

We went back into the hall, and as soon as I got the sergeant's back turned I gave Maeve the beck to come on out. As she passed the sergeant, she gave him a glare that must have rocked him back on his heels.

'Are you not going to dance,' she says to me, but instead of answering I drew her out into the dark and slipped an arm around her. We walked along for a while without saying a word. Then she gave my hand a squeeze.

'What did the sergeant want with you?'

'Ah, he was just chatting.'

'You seem to be terrible great with him.'

'I wouldn't say that. I just know him.'

'Did he say anything about me?'

'What would he say? He doesn't know you, does he?'

'Oh, the dear knows. They're a very nosy crowd, the guards. Come on back and dance.'

'No,' I said, 'I'm tired. Let's sit down.' So we sat down.

When we got back to the dance, it was near breaking up and the sergeant was gone. I was all for taking her home, but there were some cousins of hers there who said they'd take her in a trap, so I arranged to meet her the next Sunday at a dance a few miles always, and away I went singing 'The Red-Haired Girl' and whistling back at the birds.

I had an early breakfast and was off to the lake with my rod and line long before the sergeant or Hanlon or Flaherty were stirring. I spent half the day fishing and half the day daydreaming, and when I got back in the afternoon the sergeant was fit to be tied.

'Where were you all day?' says he. 'I'll report you to the superintendent for being absent without leave.'

'Oh, indeed I wasn't, Sergeant,' says I. 'I was on duty all day. I was down at the lake keeping an eye open for poachers.' It was fortunate that I had left the half dozen trout down the road on my way home.

'Poachers!' says he. 'And who ever heard of poachers on Cool Lake.'

'You never know when they might start. I took the precaution of bringing along a rod as camouflage!' I could see that he was only half convinced, but he let it go.

'Get up on your bike there,' says he. 'We have work to do.' But I told him I'd have to get something to eat first. I had such an appetite that minute that I'd have nearly eaten the sour face off himself. I downed a good meal in record time and the two of us started off.

For a couple of miles the sergeant never said a word, and I said no more. After a bit I realised we were heading up towards the mountains, a part of the world I wasn't very well acquainted with.

'Where are we off to, Sergeant?' says I.

'We're off on a job that may get you your sergeant's stripes if you play your cards right. It's that old Maurice Lynch. I have information that he's after running enough poitín to set the whole countryside drunk. He thinks he's as safe as Gibraltar, stuck up here on his mountainside, but it isn't old Sergeant Moloney he has to deal with now. Callaghan told me last night the daughter didn't know about you being in the guards.'

'That's true enough.'

'Well, maybe it's just as well you were so busy chasing after her. You'll be able to keep them in chat while I have a look around. You can pretend you came on a social call.'

I cursed my day's fishing when I realised that it was too late now to get any word to Maeve. If I'd been in the station when the sergeant first decided on this expedition, I could have sent a message through Callaghan, but here I was now on an empty bog road with the sergeant glued to my side and every stroke on the pedals bringing us nearer. There was a big push being made against poitín all through the country, and I knew it would go hard with old Lynch if he was caught.

At last we got into the mountains, and after a while we had to get down and walk, and heavy climbing it was.

'There it is now,' says the sergeant. 'We'll have to dump the bikes and take to the fields. But you go ahead and I'll follow after at a safe distance.'

Here's my chance, said I to myself, and I started hot-foot for the farmhouse. Just as I got to the gate, a fine handsome girl with red hair came out the door and leaned against the jamb, showing off her figure. I was just going to wave to her when I realised it wasn't Maeve.

'What can we do for you?' says she, looking very bold at me.

'Listen!' says I. 'This is urgent. If you have any poitín about the place, for God's sake tell me where it is till I get rid of it. There's a sergeant of the guards on his way across the fields now.'

'Poitín?' says she. 'Poitín? I seem to have heard of the stuff.'

'Look!' I said. 'This is no time for fooling. Show me where it is quick till I destroy it. God knows I'm taking enough risk.' She stretched her arms over her head and yawned.

'Is your father here?' I said.

'He is not.'

'Is Maeve?'

'She is not.'

'Well then, show me where it is quick. The sergeant will be in on top of us in a minute.'

'He'll find nothing here.'

'Very well then, I give up. But you'll be a sorry girl if your father gets six months or a year in jail.'

'Be off with you now, you have the look of a spy about you. By the big boots I'd take you for a peeler. Go on now before I let out Shep.'

I gave a sigh and turned out the gate again. The sergeant was just coming up the field, his uniform standing out against the country like a scarecrow in the corn.

'Why aren't you inside keeping them out of the way?' says he.

'There's no one there.'

'Better and better. Come on and help me now.' And he was off like a retriever from the barn. I pretended to help him in his search, but he found no more than I did.

'I'll tell you a little trick I know,' says he, and he caught up a dung-fork that was lying against the wall. 'Come out here now and I'll show you.' So I followed him out again. He went across to the heap of manure that was lying in the back yard and started to probe around it with the fork. I was just standing, admiring the fine work of a sergeant at work when there was the noise of the fork striking something and the next moment the sergeant was standing up holding a two-gallon jar. He pulled out the cork and gave the first real smile I ever saw on his face.

'Poitín!' says he, and the way he said it you'd think it was a poem. Then he whipped it behind his back and I looked round and saw Maeve's sister just coming round the corner of the house. When she saw the sergeant's uniform, she shook her fist at the two of us.

'I knew what you were,' she said. 'I knew! Let you get out of this now before my father gets back or it'll be the worse for the pair of you.'

'Be careful, young woman!' says the sergeant. 'It is a very dangerous thing to obstruct a garda officer in the discharge of his duty. We are here in search of illicit spirits, and if there is any on the premises it is wiser to tell us now.'

I was leaning against the door of the barn, looking out over the Mayo mountains, and wondering how long would poor old Lynch get at the District Court when what should I see peeping up over the hedge but another red head. And this time it was Maeve sure enough. She had been there all the time watching every move. She gave me a wicked glare. I winked back. The sergeant was standing with his back turned to her, rocking from his heels to his toes playing cat-and-mouse with the sister, and waggling the jar gently behind his back. There wasn't a prouder sergeant on the soil of Ireland that minute.

I could see that Maeve wasn't quite sure whether I was just a pal of the sergeant's that came out to keep him company, or a garda on duty, and she kept glancing from me to the jar that the sergeant was so busy hiding. She seemed to be asking me a question with her eyes. As there wasn't anything I could do to help her, I gave another wink and a big grin. She looked hard at me, then ducked out of sight behind the hedge. I was just beginning to wonder what had happened to her when she stood up straight, and my heart nearly stopped when I saw the big lump of rock she had in her fist. I'm not a very narrow-minded man, and I had no particular regard for the sergeant, but I wasn't going to have him murdered in cold blood before my eyes. If a thing like that came out at the inquest it would look very bad on my record. I was in two minds whether to shout out or not, weighing the trouble Maeve and her family would get into if I did against the trouble I'd get into if I didn't, when she drew back her arm, took wicked and deliberate aim, and let fly. I closed my eyes tight and turned away. When I heard a scream of agony from the sergeant, I closed them even tighter, but I opened them again when I heard what he was shouting.

'Blast it! Blast it! Blast it to hell!' he was roaring, and then I saw the heap of broken crockery at his feet. The sister was in kinks of laughter and there wasn't a sign of Maeve. There was a most delightful smell of the very best poitín on the air, and when the sergeant threw the handle of the jar on the ground in rage, I realised that it was the jar and not the sergeant's head that had received the blow. I burst out laughing.

'Who did that?' he shouted at me. 'Who did that, you grinning imbecile?' But I shook my head.

'I was just daydreaming,' I said. 'I didn't see a thing.'

'You'll pay for this!' he shouted. 'You'll pay dearly for this, you inefficient lout! Dereliction of duty! Gross imbecility! Crass stupidity! I'll have the coat off your back for this day's work!' Of course the poor man didn't know what he was saying, but in a way I was nearly sorry for him. He was so sure that he had the case all sewn up. But now, without the contents of the jar, any chance of a prosecution was ballooned from the beginning. The law requires very strict proof in these matters.

The sergeant and myself searched all through the farm that day. And every day for a week afterwards Flaherty and Hanlon and myself searched it again. But it was labour in vain. It was great weather, though, and after the first day I managed to get Maeve to join me. I had a terrible job persuading her that all guards aren't as bad as she thought, and that the sergeant was quite exceptional. Fortunately, Flaherty and Hanlon were in no great hurry to get the searching finished, so I had plenty of time to devote to persuading her. For some reason, old Lynch didn't seem to care if we searched till doomsday, and himself and myself struck up a great friendship when I told him about my conversation with Maeve's sister, Mary. So that when Maeve agreed to marry me, he put up no objection.

The sergeant did his level best to have me drummed out of the guards for marrying a poitín-maker's daughter, but, as I pointed out to the superintendent, there was no proof that Maurice Lynch ever ran a drop of poitín, and even if he did, wouldn't a garda in the family be the greatest deterrent against illicit distilling? The superintendent saw my point, but

I'm not so sure that I was right. I've often said that my father-in-law makes the smoothest run of mountain dew it has ever been my luck to taste.

It was just as well the sergeant was moved soon after. He was very bitter about the broken jar and would have stopped at nothing to get a conviction. Things have been very quiet and peaceful since he left, and crime has practically disappeared from the district.

Sir Dominick's Bargain

by J. Sheridan Le Fanu

In the early autumn of the year 1838, business called me to the south of Ireland. The weather was delightful, the scenery and the people were new to me, and sending my luggage on by the mail-coach route in charge of a servant, I hired a serviceable nag at a posting-house, and, full of the curiosity of an explorer, I commenced a leisurely journey of five-and-twenty miles on horseback, by sequestered crossroads, to my place of destination. By bog and hill, by plain and ruined castle, and many a winding stream, my picturesque road led me.

I had started late, and having made a little more than half my journey, I was thinking of making a short halt at the next convenient place, and letting my horse have a rest and feed, and making some provision also for the comforts of the rider.

It was about four o'clock when the road, ascending a gradual steep, found a passage through a rocky gorge between the abrupt termination of a range of mountains to my left and a rocky hill, that turned dark and sudden at my right. Below me lay a little thatched village, under a long line of gigantic beech-trees, through the boughs of which the lowly chimneys sent up their thin turf-smoke. To my left, stretched away for miles, ascending the mountain range I have mentioned, a wild park, through whose sward and ferns the rock broke, time-worn and lichen-stained. This park was studded with straggling wood which thickened to something like a forest, behind and beyond the little village I was approaching, clothing the irregular ascent of the hillsides with beautiful, and in some places discoloured foliage.

As you descend, the road winds slightly, with the grey park-wall built of loose stone, and mantled here and there with ivy, at its left, and crosses a shallow ford; and as I approached the village, through breaks in the woodlands, I caught glimpses of the long front of an old ruined house, placed among the trees, about half-way up the picturesque mountain side.

The solitude and melancholy of this ruin piqued my curiosity, and when I had reached the rude thatched public house, with the sign of St Colmcille, with robes, mitre and crozier displayed over its lintel, having seen to my horse and made a good meal myself on a rasher and eggs, I began to think again on the wooded park and the ruinous house, and resolved on a ramble of half an hour among its sylvan solitudes.

The name of the place, I found, was Dunoran; and beside the gate a stile admitted to the grounds through which, with a pensive enjoyment, I began to saunter towards the dilapidated mansion.

A long grass-grown road, with many turns and windings, led up to the old house, under the shadow of the wood.

The road, as it approached the house, skirted the edge of a precipitous glen, clothed with hazel, dwarf-oak and thorn, and the silent house stood with its wide open half-door facing this dark ravine, the further edge of which was crowned with towering forest; and great trees stood about the house and its deserted courtyard and stable.

I walked in and looked about me, through passages overgrown with nettles and weeds; from room to room with ceilings rotted, and here and there a great beam dark and worn, with tendrils of ivy trailing over it. The tall walls with rotten plaster were stained and mouldy, and in some rooms the remains of decayed wainscoting crazily swung to and fro. The almost sashless windows were darkened also with ivy, and about the tall chimneys the jackdaws were wheeling, while from the huge trees that overhung the glen in sombre masses at the other side, the rooks kept up ceaseless cawing.

As I walked through these melancholy passages – peeping only into some of the rooms, for the flooring was quite gone in the middle, and bowed down toward the centre, and the house was very nearly unroofed, a state of things which made the exploration a little critical – I began to wonder why so grand a house, in the midst of scenery so picturesque, had been permitted to go to decay; I dreamed of the hospitalities of which it had long ago been the rallying place, and I thought what a scene of Redgauntlet revelries it might disclose at midnight.

The great staircase was of oak, which had stood the weather wonderfully, and I sat down upon its steps, musing vaguely on the transitoriness of all things under the sun.

Except for the hoarse and distant clamour of the rooks, hardly audible where I sat, no sound broke the profound stillness of the spot. Such a sense of solitude I have seldom experienced before. The air was stirless, there was not even the rustle of a withered leaf along the passage. It was oppressive. The tall trees that stood close about the building darkened it, and added something of awe to the melancholy of the scene.

In this mood I heard, with an unpleasant surprise, close to me, a voice that was drawling and, I fancied, sneering, repeat the words: 'Food for worms, dead and rotten; God over all.'

There was a small window in the wall, here very thick, which had been built up, and in the dark recess of this, deep in the shadow, I now saw a sharp-featured man, sitting with his feet dangling. His keen eyes were fixed on me, and he was smiling cynically, and before I had well recovered my surprise, he repeated the distich:

> If death was a thing that money could buy,
> The rich they would live, and the poor they would die.

'It was a grand house in its day, sir,' he continued, 'Dunoran House, and the Sarsfields. Sir Dominick Sarsfield was the last of the old stock. He lost his life not six foot away from where you are sitting.'

As he thus spoke he let himself down, with a little jump, on to the ground.

He was a dark-faced, sharp-featured, little hunchback, and had a walking stick in his hand, with the end of which he pointed to a rusty stain in the plaster of the wall.

'Do you mind that mark, sir?' he asked.

'Yes,' I said, standing up, and looking at it, with a curious anticipation of something worth hearing.

'That's about seven or eight feet from the ground, sir, and you'll not guess what it is.'

'I dare say not,' said I, 'unless it is a stain from the weather.'

''Tis nothing so lucky, sir,' he answered, with the same cynical smile and a wag of head, still pointing at the mark with his stick. 'That's a splash of brains and blood. It's there this hundred years; and it will never leave while the wall stands.'

'He was murdered, then?'

'Worse than that, sir,' he answered.

'He killed himself, perhaps?'

'Worse than that, itself, this cross between us and harm! I'm oulder than I look, sir; you wouldn't guess my years.'

He became silent, and looked at me, evidently inviting a guess.

'Well, I should guess you to be about five-and-twenty.'

He laughed and took a pinch of snuff, and said:

'I'm that, your honour, and something to the back of it. I was seventy last Candlemas. You should not 'a' thought that, to look at me.'

'Upon my word I should not; I can hardly believe it even now. Still, you don't remember Sir Dominick Sarsfield's death?' I said, glancing up at the ominous stain on the wall.

'No, sir, that was a long while before I was born. But my grandfather was butler here long ago, and many a time I heard tell how Sir Dominick came by his death. There was no masther in the great house ever sinst that happened. But there was two servants in care of it, and my aunt was one o' them; and she kep me here wid her till I was nine year old, and she was lavin' the place to go to Dublin; and from that time it was let to go down. The wind sthript the roof, and the rain rotted the timber, and little by little, in sixty years' time, it kem to what you see. But I have a likin' for it still, for the sake of ould times; and I never come this way but I take a look in. I don't think it's many more times I'll be turnin' to see the ould place, for I'll be undher the sod myself before long.'

'You'll outlive younger people,' I said.

And, quitting that trite subject, I ran on:

'I don't wonder that you like this old place; it is a beautiful spot, such noble trees.'

'I wish ye seen the glin when the nuts is ripe; they're the sweetest nuts in all Ireland, I think,' he rejoined, and with a practical sense of the picturesque. 'You'd fill your pockets while you'd be lookin' about you.'

'These are very fine old woods,' I remarked. 'I have not seen any in Ireland I thought so beautiful.'

'Eiah! your honour, the woods about here is nothing to what they wor. All the mountains along here was wood when my father was a garsún, and Murroa Wood was the grandest of them all. All oak mostly, and all cut down as bare as the road. Not one left here that's fit to compare with them. Which way did your honour come hither – from Limerick?'

'No. Killaloe.'

'Well, then, you passed the ground where Murroa Wood was in former times. You kem undher Lisnavourra, the steep knob of a hill about a mile above the village here. 'Twas near there that Murroa Wood was, and 'twas there Sir Dominick Sarsfield first met the devil, the Lord between us and harm, and a bad meeting it was for him and his.'

I had become interested in the adventure which had occurred in the very scenery which had so greatly attracted me, and my new acquaintance, the little hunchback, was easily entreated to tell me the story, and spoke thus, so soon as we had each returned to his seat:

'It was a fine estate when Sir Dominick came into it; and grand doings there was entirely, feasting and fiddling, free quarters for all the pipers in the counthry round, and a welcome for every one that liked to come. There was wine, by the hogshead, for the quality; and poitín enough to set a town a-fire, and beer and cidher enough to float a navy, for the boys and girls, and the likes of me. It was kep' up the best part of a month, till the weather broke, and the rain spoilt the sod for the moneen jigs, and the fair of Allybally Killudeen comin' on they wor obliged to give over their diversion, and attind to the pigs.

'But Sir Dominick was only beginnin' when they wor lavin' off. There was no way of gettin' rid of his money and estates he did not try – what with drinkin', dicin', racin', cards, and all sorts, it was not many years before the estates wor in debt, and Sir Dominick a distressed man. He showed a bold front to the world as long as he could; and then he sould off his dogs, and the most of his horses, and gev out he was going to thravel in France, and the like; and so off with him for a while and no one in these parts heard tale or tidings of him for two or three years. Till at last, quite unexpected, one night there comes a rapping at the big kitchen window. It was past ten o'clock, and old Connor Hanlon, the butler, my grandfather, was sittin' by the fire alone, warming his shins over it. There was a keen east wind blowing along the mountains that night, and whistling cowld enough through the tops of the trees, and soundin' lonesome through the long chimneys.

(And the storyteller glanced up at the nearest stack visible from his seat.)

'So he wasn't quite sure of the knockin' at the window, and up he gets, and sees his master's face.

'My grandfather was glad to see him safe, for it was a long time since there was any news of him; but he was sorry, too, for it was a changed place and only himself and old Juggy Broadrick in charge of the house, and a man in the stables, and it was a poor thing to see him comin' back to his own like that.

'He shook Con by the hand, and says he:

'"I came here to say a word to you. I left my horse with Dick in the stable; I may want him again before morning, or I may never want him."

'And with that he turns into the big kitchen, and draws a stool, and sits down to take an air of the fire.

'"Sit down, Connor, opposite me, and listen to what I tell

you, and don't be afeard to say what you think."

'He spoke all the time lookin' into the fire, with his hands stretched over it and a tired man he looked.

'"An' why should I be afeard, Masther Dominick?" says my grandfather. "Yourself was a good masther to me, and so was your father, rest his soul, before you, and I'll say the truth, and dar' the devil, and more than that, for any Sarsfield of Dunoran, much less yourself, and a good right I'd have."

'"It's all over with me, Con," says Sir Dominick.

'"Heaven forbid!" says my grandfather.

'"'Tis past praying for," says Sir Dominick. "The last guinea's gone; the ould place will follow it. It must be sould, and I'm come here, I don't know why, like a ghost to have a last look round me, and go off in the dark again."

'And with that he tould him to be sure, in case he should hear of his death, to give the oak box, in the closet off his room to his cousin, Pat Sarsfield, in Dublin, and the sword and pistols his grandfather carried in Aughrim, and two or three trifling things of the kind.

'And says he, "Con, they say if the divil gives you money overnight, you'll find nothing but a bagful of pebbles, and chips, and nutshells, in the morning. If I thought he played fair, I'm in the humour to make a bargain with him tonight."

'"Lord forbid!" says my grandfather, standing up with a start, and crossing himself.

'"They say the country's full of men, listin' sogers for the king o' France. If I light on one o' them, I'll not refuse his offer. How contrary things goes! How long is it since me and Captain Waller fought the jewel at New Castle?"

'"Six years, Masther Dominick, and ye broke his thigh with the bullet the first shot."

'"I did, Con," says he, "and I wish, instead, he had shot me through the heart. Have you any whiskey?"

'My grandfather took it out of the buffet, and the masther pours out some into a bowl, and drank it off.

'"I'll go out and have a look at my horse," says he, standing up. There was a sort of a stare in his eyes, as he pulled his riding-cloak about him, as if there was something bad in his thoughts.

'"Sure, I won't be a minute running out myself to the stable, and looking after the horse for you myself," says my grandfather.

'"I'm not goin' to the stable," says Sir Dominick; "I may as well tell you, for I see you found it out already – I'm goin' across the deerpark; if I come back you'll see me in an hour's time. But, anyhow, you'd better not follow me, for if you do I'll shoot you, and that'd be a bad ending to our friendship."

'And with that he walks down the passage here, and turns the key in the side door at that end of it, and out wid him on the sod into the moonlight and the cowld wind; and my grandfather seen him walkin' hard towards the park wall, and then he comes in and closes the door with a heavy heart.

'Sir Dominick stopped to think when he got to the middle of the deerpark, for he had not made up his mind when he left the house and the whiskey did not clear his head, only it gev him courage.

'He did not feel the cowld wind now, nor fear death, nor think much of anything, but the shame and fall of the old family.

'And he made up his mind, if no better thought came to him between that and there, so soon as he came to Murroa Wood, he'd hang himself from one of the oak branches with his cravat.

'It was a bright moonlight night, there was just a bit of a cloud driving across the moon now and then, but, only for that, as light a'most as day.

'Down he goes, right for the wood of Murroa. It seemed to him every step he took was as three, and it was no time till he was among the big oak-trees with their roots spreading from one to another, and their branches stretching overhead like the timbers of a naked roof, and the moon shining down through them, and casting shadows thick on the ground as black as my shoe.

'He was sobering a bit by this time, and he slacked his pace, and he thought 'twould be better to list in the French king's army, and thry what that might do for him, for he knew a man might take his own life any time, but it would puzzle him to take it back again when he liked.

'Just as he made up his mind not to make away with himself, what should he hear but a step clinkin' along the dry ground under the trees, and soon he sees a grand gentleman right before him comin' up to meet him.

'He was a handsome young man like himself, and he wore a cocked hat with gold lace round it, such as officers wear on their coats, and he had on a dress the same as French officers wore in them times.

'He stopped opposite Sir Dominick, and he cum to a standstill also.

'The two gentlemen took off their hats to one another, and says the stranger:

'"I am recruiting, sir," says he, "for my sovereign, and you'll find my money won't turn into pebbles, chips and nutshells, by tomorrow."

'At the same time he pulls out a big purse of gold.

'The minute he sets eyes on that gentleman, Sir Dominick had his own opinion of him; and at those words he felt the very hair standing up on his head.

'"Don't be afraid," says he, "the money won't burn you. If it proves honest gold, and if it prospers with you, I'm willing to make a bargain. This is the last day of February," says he; "I'll serve you seven years, and at the end of that time you shall serve me, and I'll come for you when the seven years is over, when the clock turns the minute between February and March; and the first of March ye'll come away with me, or never. You'll not find me a bad master, any more than a bad servant. I love my own; and I command all the pleasures and the glory of the world. The bargain dates from this day, and the lease is out at midnight on the last day I told you; and in the year" – he told him the year, it was easy reckoned, but I forget it – "and if you'd rather wait," he says, "for eight months and twenty-eight days, before you sign the writin', you may, if you meet me here. But I can't do a great deal for you in the meantime; and if you don't sign then, all you get from up to that time, will vanish away, and you'll be just as you are tonight, and ready to hang yourself on the first tree you meet."

'Well, the end of it was, Sir Dominick chose to wait, and

he came back to the house with a big bag full of money, as round as your hat a'most.

'My grandfather was glad enough, you may be sure, to see the master safe and sound again so soon. Into the kitchen he bangs again, and swings the bag o' money on the table; and he stands up straight, and heaves up his shoulders like a man that has just got shut of his load; and he looks at the bag, and my grandfather looks at him, and from him to it, and back again. Sir Dominick looked as white as a sheet, and says he:

'"I don't know, Con, what's in it; it's the heaviest load I ever carried."

'He seemed shy of openin' the bag; and he made my grandfather heap up a roaring fire of turf and wood, and then, at last, he opens it, and sure enough, 'twas stuffed full of golden guineas, bright and new, as if they were only that minute out o' the Mint.

'Sir Dominick made my grandfather sit at his elbow while he counted every guinea in the bag.

'When he was done countin', and it wasn't far from daylight when that time came, Sir Dominick made my grandfather swear not to tell a word about it. And a close secret it was for many a day after.

'When the eight months and twenty-eight days were pretty near spent and ended, Sir Dominick returned to the house here with a troubled mind, in doubt what was best to be done, and no one alive but my grandfather knew anything about the matter, and he not half what had happened.

'As the day drew near, towards the end of October, Sir Dominick grew only more and more troubled in mind.

'One time he made up his mind to have no more to say to such things, nor to speak again with the like of them he met with in the wood of Murroa. Then, again, his heart failed him when he thought of his debts, and he not knowing where to turn. Then, only a week before the day, everything began to go wrong with him. One man wrote from London to say that Sir Dominick paid three thousand pounds to the wrong man, and must pay it over again; another, in Dublin, denied the payment of the thunderin' big bill, and Sir Dominick could nowhere find the receipt, and so on, wid fifty other things as bad.

'Well, by the time the night of the twenty-eighth of October came round, he was a'most ready to lose his senses with all the demands that was risin' up agains' him on all sides, and nothing to meet them but the help of the one dhreadful friend he had to depind on at night in the oak-wood down there below.

'So there was nothing for it but to go through with the business that was begun already, and about the same hour as he went last, he takes off the little crucifix he wore round his neck, for he was a Catholic, and his gospel, and his bit of the thrue cross that he had in a locket, for since he took the money from the Evil One he was growin' frightful in himself, and got all he could to guard him from the power of the devil. But to-night, for this life, he daren't take them with him. So he gives them into my grandfather's hands without a word, only he looked as white as a sheet o' paper; and he takes his hat and sword, and telling my grandfather to watch for him, away he goes, to try what would come of it.

'It was a fine still night, and the moon – not so bright, though, now as the first time – was shinin' over heath and rock, and down on the lonesome oak-wood below him.

'His heart beat thick as he drew near it. There was not a sound, not even the distant bark of a dog from the village behind him. There was not a lonesomer spot in the country round, and if it wasn't for his debts and losses that was drivin' him on half mad, in spite of his fears for his soul and his hopes of paradise, and all his good angel was whisperin' in his ear, he would 'a' turned back, and sent for his clargy, and made his confession and his penance, and changed his ways, and led a good life, for he was frightened enough to have done a great dale.

'Softer and slower he stept as he got, once more, in undher the big branches of the oak-trees; and when he got in a bit, near where he met with the bad spirit before, he stopped and looked round him, and felt himself, every bit, turning cowld as a dead man, and you may be sure he did not feel much bether when he seen the same man steppin' from behind the big tree that was touchin' his elbow a'most.

'"You found the money good," says he, "but it was not

enough. No matter, you shall have enough and to spare. I'll see after your luck and I'll give you a hint whenever it can serve you; and any time you want to see me you have only to come down here, and call my face to mind, and wish me present. You shan't owe a shilling by the end of the year, and you shall never miss the right card, the best throw, and the winning horse. Are you willing?"

'The young gentleman's voice almost stuck in his throat, and his hair was rising on his head, but he did get out a word or two to signify that he consented and with that the Evil One handed him a needle, and bid him give him three drops of blood from his arm; and he took them in the cup of an acorn, and gave him a pen, and bid him write some words that he repeated, and that Sir Dominick did not understand, on two thin slips of parchment. He took one himself and the other he sunk in Sir Dominick's arm at the place where he drew the blood, and he closed the flesh over it. And that's as true as you're sittin' there!

'Well, Sir Dominick went home. He was a frightened man, and well he might be. But in a little time he began to grow aisier in his mind. Anyhow, he got out of debt very quick, and money came tumbling in to make him richer, and everything he took in hand prospered, and he never made a wager, or played a game, but he won; and for all that, there was not a poor man on the estate that was no happier than Sir Dominick.

'So he took again to his old ways; for, when the money came back, all came back, and there were hounds and horses, and wine galore, and no end of company, and grand doin's, and diversion, up here at the great house. And some said Sir Dominick was thinkin' of gettin' married; and more said he wasn't. But, anyhow, there was somethin' troublin' him more than common, and so one night, unknownst to all, away he goes to the lonesome oak-wood. It was something, maybe, my grandfather thought was troublin' him about a beautiful young lady he was jealous of, and mad in love with her. But that was only a guess.

'Well, when Sir Dominick got into the wood this time, he grew more in dread than ever; and he was on the point of turnin' and lavin' the place, when who should he see, close

beside him, but my gentleman, seated on a big stone undher
one of the trees. In place of looking the fine young gentleman
in gold lace and grand clothes he appeared before, he was
now in rags, he looked twice the size he had been, and his face
smutted with soot, and he had a murtherin' big steel hammer,
as heavy as a half-hundhred, with a handle a yard long, across
his knees. It was so dark under the tree, he did not see him
quite clear for some time.

'He stood up, and he looked awful tall entirely. And what
passed between them in that discourse my grandfather never
heered. But Sir Dominick was as black as night afterwards,
and hadn't a laugh for anything nor a word a'most for any
one, and he only grew worse and worse, and darker and darker. And now this thing, whatever it was, used to come to him
of its own accord, whether he wanted it or no; sometimes in
one shape, and sometimes at his side by night when he'd be
ridin' home alone, until at last he lost heart altogether and sent
for the priest.

'The priest was with him a long time, and when he heered
the whole story, he rode off all the way for the bishop, and the
bishop came here to the great house next day, and he gev Sir
Dominick a good advice. He tould him he must give over
dicin', and swearin' and drinkin' and all bad company, and
live a vartuous steady life until the seven years' bargain was
out, and if the divil didn't come for him the minute afther the
stroke of twelve the first morning of the month of March, he
was safe out of the bargain. There was not more than eight or
ten months to run now before the seven years wor out, and he
lived all the time according to the bishop's advice, as strict as
if he was "in retreat".

'Well you may guess he felt quare enough when the
mornin' of the twenty-eighth of February came.

'The priest came up by appointment, and Sir Dominick
and his raverence wor together in the room you see there, and
kep' up their prayers together till the clock struck twelve, and
a good hour after, and not a sign of a disturbance, nor nothing
came near them, and the priest slep' that night in the house in
the room next to Sir Dominick's, and all went over as com-
fortable as could be, and they shook hands and kissed like two

comrades after winning a battle.

'So now, Sir Dominick thought he might as well have a pleasant evening, and after all his fastin' and prayin'; and he sent round to half a dozen of the neighbouring gentlemen to come and dine with him, and his raverence stayed and dined also, and a roarin' bowl o' punch they had and no end o' wine, and the swearin' and dice, and cards and guineas changin' hands, and songs and stories that wouldn't do any one good to hear, and the priest slipped away, when he seen the turn things was takin', and it was not far from the stroke of twelve when Sir Dominick, sitting at the head of his table, swears, "This is the best first of March I ever sat down with my friends."

'"It ain't the first of March," says Mr Hiffernan of Ballyvoureen. He was a scholard, and always kep' an almanack.

'"What is it then?" said Sir Dominick, startin' up, and dhroppin' the ladle into the bowl, and starin' at him as if he had two heads.

'"'Tis the twenty-ninth of February, leap year," says he. And just as they were talkin', the clock strikes twelve; and my grandfather, who was half asleep in a chair by the fire in the hall, openin' his eyes, sees a short square fellow with a cloak on, and long black hair bushin' out from under his hat, standin' just there where you see the bit o' light again' the wall.'

(My hunchback friend pointed with his stick to a little patch of red sunset light that relieved the deepening shadow of the passage.)

'"Tell your master," says he, in an awful voice, like the growl of a baist, "that I'm here by appointment, and expect him downstairs this minute."

'Up goes my grandfather, by these very steps you are sittin' on.

'"Tell him I can't come down yet," says Sir Dominick, and he turns to the company in the room, and says he with a cold sweat shinin' on his face, "For God's sake, gentlemen, will any of you jump from the window and bring the priest here?"

One looked at another and no one knew what to make of it, and in the meantime, up comes my grandfather again, and says he, tremblin', "He says, sir, unless you go down to him, he'll come up to you."

'"I don't understand this, gentlemen, I'll see what it means," says Sir Dominick trying to put a face on it, and walkin' out o' the room like a man through the pressroom, with the hangman waitin' for him outside. Down the stairs he comes, and two or three of the gentlemen peeping over the banisters, to see. My grandfather was walking six or eight steps behind him, and he seen the stranger take a stride out to meet Sir Dominick, and catch him up in his arms, and whirl his head against the wall, and wi' that the hall-door flies open, and out goes the candles, and the turf and wood-ashes flyin' with the wind out o' the hall-fire, ran in a drift o' sparks along the floor by his feet.

'Down runs the gentlemen. Bang goes the hall-door. Some comes runnin' up, and more runnin' down, with lights. It was all over with Sir Dominick. They lifted up the corpse, and put its shoulders again' the wall; but there was not a gasp left in him. He was cowld and stiffenin' already.

'Pat Donovan was comin' up to the great house late that night and after he passed the little brook, that the carriage track up to the house crosses, and about fifty steps to this side of it, his dog, that was by his side, makes a sudden wheel, and springs over the wall, and sets up a yowlin' inside you'd hear a mile away; and that minute two men passed him by in silence, goin' down from the house, one of them short and square, and the other like Sir Dominick in shape, but there was little light under the trees where he was, and they looked only like shadows; and as they passed him by he could not hear the sound of their feet and he drew back to the wall frightened; and when he got up to the great house, he found all in confusion, and the master's body, with the head smashed to pieces, lying just on *that spot*.'

The narrator stood up and indicated with the point of his stick the exact site of the body, and, as I looked, the shadow deepened, the red stain of sunlight vanished from the wall, and the sun had gone behind the distant hill of New Castle, leaving the haunted scene in the deep grey of darkening twilight.

So I and the storyteller parted, not without good wishes

on both sides, and a little 'tip' which seemed not unwelcome, from me.

It was dusk and the moon up by the time I reached the village, remounted my nag, and looked my last on the scene of the terrible legend of Dunoran.

TRINKET'S COLT

by Somerville and Ross

IT WAS PETTY SESSIONS in Skebawn, a cold grey day of February. A case of trespass had dragged its burden of cross summonses and cross swearing far into the afternoon, and when I left the bench my head was singing from the bellowing of the attorneys, and the smell of their clients was heavy upon my palate.

The street still testified to the fact that it was market day, and I evaded with difficulty the sinuous course of carts full of soddenly screwed people, and steered an equally devious one for myself among the groups anchored round the doors of the public houses. Skebawn possesses, among its legion of public houses, one establishment which timorously, and almost imperceptibly, proffers tea to the thirsty. I turned in there, as was my custom on court days, and found the little dingy den, known as the Ladies' Coffee-room, in the occupancy of my friend, Mr Florence McCarthy Knox, who was drinking strong tea and eating buns with serious simplicity. It was a first and quite unexpected glimpse of that domesticity that has now become a marked feature in his character.

'You're the very man I wanted to see,' I said as I sat down

beside him at the oilcloth-covered table; 'a man I know in England who is not much of a judge of character has asked me to buy him a four-year-old down here, and as I should rather be stuck by a friend than a dealer, I wish you'd take over the job.'

Flurry poured himself out another cup of tea, and dropped three lumps of sugar into it in silence.

Finally he said, 'There isn't a four-year-old in this county that I'd be seen dead with at a pig fair.'

This was discouraging, from the premier authority on horseflesh in the district.

'But it isn't six weeks since you told me you had the finest filly in your stables that was ever foaled in the County Cork,' I protested; 'What's wrong with her?'

'Oh, is it that filly?' said Mr Knox with a lenient smile; 'She's gone these three weeks from me. I swapped her and six pounds for a three-year-old Ironmonger colt, and after that I swapped the colt and nineteen pounds for that Bandon horse I rode last week at your place, and after that again I sold the Bandon horse for seventy-five pounds to old Welply, and I had to give him back a couple of sovereigns luck-money. You see I did pretty well with the filly after all.'

'Yes, yes – oh, rather,' I assented, as one dizzily accepts the propositions of a bimetallist; 'and you don't know of anything else – ?'

The room in which we were seated was closely screened from the shop by a door with a muslin-curtained window in it; several of the panes were broken, and at this juncture two voices that had for some time carried on a discussion forced themselves upon our attention.

'Begging your pardon for contradicting you, ma'am,' said the voice of Mrs McDonald, proprietress of the teashop, and a leading light in Skebawn Dissenting circles, shrilly tremulous with indignation, 'if the servants I recommend you won't stop with you, it's no fault of mine. If respectable young girls are set picking grass out of your gravel, in place of their proper work, certainly they will give warning!'

The voice that replied struck me as being a notable one, well-bred and imperious.

'When I take a bare-footed slut out of a cabin, I don't expect her to dictate to me what her duties are!'

Flurry jerked up his chin in a noiseless laugh. 'It's my grandmother!' he whispered. 'I bet you Mrs McDonald don't get much change out of her!'

'If I set her to clean the pigsty I expect her to obey me,' continued the voice in accents that would have made me clean forty pigsties had she desired me to do so.

'Very well, ma'am,' retorted Mrs McDonald, 'if that's the way you treat your servants, you needn't come here again looking for them. I consider your conduct is neither that of a lady or a Christian!'

'Don't you indeed?' replied Flurry's grandmother. 'Well, your opinion doesn't really distress me, for, to tell you the truth, I don't think you're much of a judge.'

'Didn't I tell you she'd score?' murmured Flurry, who was by this time applying his eye to the hole in the muslin curtain. 'She's off,' he went on, returning to his tea. 'She's a great character! She's eighty-three if she's a day, and she's as sound on her legs as a three-year-old! Did you see the old shandryhan of hers in the street a while ago, and a fellow on the box with a red beard on him like Robinson Crusoe? That old mare that was on the near side – Trinket her name is – is mighty near clean bred. I can tell you her foals are worth a bit of money.'

I had heard of old Mrs Knox of Aussolas; indeed, I had seldom dined out in the neighbourhood without hearing some new story of her and her remarkable ménage, but it had not yet been my privilege to meet her.

'Well, now,' went on Flurry in his slow voice, 'I'll tell you a thing that's just come into my head. My grandmother promised me a foal of Trinket's the day I was one-and-twenty, and that's five years ago, and deuce a one I've got from her yet. You never were at Aussolas? No, you were not. Well, I tell you the place there is like a circus with horses. She had a couple of score of them running wild in the woods, like deer.'

'Oh, come,' I said, 'I'm a bit of a liar myself – '

'Well, she has a dozen of them anyhow, rattling good colts too, some of them, but they might as well be donkeys, for all the good they are to me or to anyone. It's not once in three years she sells one, and there she has them walking after her for bits of sugar, like a lot of dirty lapdogs,' ended Flurry with disgust.

'Well, what's your plan? Do you want me to make her a bid for one of the lapdogs?'

'I was thinking,' replied Flurry, with great deliberation, 'that my birthday's this week, and maybe I could work a four-year-old colt of Trinket's she has out of her in honour of the occasion.'

'And sell your grandmother's birthday present to me?'

'Just that, I suppose,' answered Flurry with a slow wink.

A few days afterwards a letter from Mr Knox informed me that he had 'squared the old lady' and it would be 'all right about the colt'. He further told me that Mrs Knox had been good enough to offer me, with him, a day's snipe shooting on the celebrated Aussolas bogs, and he proposed to drive me there the following Monday, if convenient. Most people found it convenient to shoot the Aussolas snipe bog when they got the chance.

Eight o'clock on the following Monday morning saw Flurry, myself, and a groom packed into a dogcart, with port-manteaus, gun-cases, and two rampant red setters.

It was a long drive, twelve miles at least, and a very cold one. We passed through long tracts of pasture country, fraught, for Flurry, with memories of runs, which were record-ed for me, fence by fence, in every one of which the biggest dog-fox in the country had gone to ground, with not two feet – measured accurately on the handle of the whip – between him and the leading hound; through bogs that imperceptibly melted into lakes, and finally down and down into the valley, where the fir trees of Aussolas clustered darkly round a glittering lake, and all but hid the grey roofs and pointed gables of Aussolas Castle.

'There's a nice stretch of demesne for you,' remarked Flurry, pointing downwards with the whip, 'and one little old woman holding it all in the heel of her fist. Well able to hold it she is, too, and always was, and she'll live twenty years yet, if it's only to spite the whole lot of us, and when all's said and done goodness knows how she'll leave it!'

'It strikes me you were lucky to keep her up to her promise about the colt,' I said.

Flurry administered a composing kick to the ceaseless strivings of the red setters under the seat.

'I used to be rather a pet with her,' he said, after a pause; 'but mind you, I haven't got him yet, and if she gets any notion I want to sell him I'll never get him, so say nothing about the business to her.'

The tall gates of Aussolas shrieked on their hinges as they admitted us, and shut with a clang behind us, in the faces of an old mare and a couple of young horses, who, foiled in their break for the excitement of the outer world, turned and galloped defiantly on either side of us. Flurry's admirable cob hammered on, regardless of all things save his duty.

'He's the only one I have that I'd trust myself here with,' said his master, flicking him approvingly with the whip; 'there are plenty of people afraid to come here at all, and when my grandmother goes out driving, she has a boy on the box with a basket full of stones to peg at them. Talk of the dickens, here she is herself!'

A short, upright woman was approaching, preceded by a white woolly dog with sore eyes and a bark like a tin trumpet; we both got out of the trap and advanced to meet the lady of the manor.

I may summarise her attire by saying that she looked as if she had robbed a scarecrow; her face was small and incongruously refined, the skinny hand that she extended to me had the grubby tan that bespoke the professional gardener, and was decorated with a magnificent diamond ring. On her head was a massive purple velvet bonnet.

'I am very glad to meet you, Major Yeates,' she said with an old-fashioned precision of utterance; 'your grandfather was a dancing partner of mine in old days at the Castle, when he was a handsome young aide-de-camp there, and I was – you may judge for yourself what I was.'

She ended with a startling little hoot of laughter, and I was aware that she quite realised the world's opinion of her, and was indifferent to it.

Our way to the bogs took us across Mrs Knox's home

farm, and through a large field in which several young horses were grazing.

'There now, that's my fellow,' said Flurry, pointing to a fine-looking colt, 'the chestnut with the white diamond on his forehead. He'll run into three figures before he's done, but we'll not tell that to the old lady!'

The famous Aussolas bogs were as full of snipe as usual, and a good deal fuller of water than any bogs I had ever shot before. I was on my day, and Flurry was not, and as he is ordinarily an infinitely better snipe shot than I, I felt at peace with the world and all men as we walked back, wet through, at five o'clock.

The sunset had waned, and a big white moon was making the eastern tower of Aussolas look like a thing in a fairy tale or a play when we arrived at the hall door. An individual, whom I recognised as the Robinson Crusoe coachman, admitted us all to a hall, the like of which one does not often see. The walls were panelled with dark oak up to the gallery that ran around three sides of it, the balusters of the wide staircase were heavily carved, and blackened portraits of Flurry's ancestors on the spindle side stared sourly down on their descendants as he tramped upstairs with the bog mould on his hobnailed boots.

We had just changed into dry clothes when Robinson Crusoe shoved his red beard round the corner of the door, with the information that the mistress said we were to stay for dinner. My heart sank. It was then barely half past five. I said something about having no evening clothes and having to get home early.

'Sure the dinner'll be ready in another half hour,' said Robinson Crusoe, joining hospitably in the conversation; 'and as for the evening clothes – God bless ye!'

The door closed behind him.

'Never mind,' said Flurry, 'I dare say you'll be glad enough to eat another dinner by the time you get home.' He laughed again when I asked for an explanation.

Old Mrs Knox received us in the library, where she was seated by a roaring turf fire, which lit the room a good deal more effectively than the pair of candles that stood beside her in tall silver candlesticks. Ceaseless and implacable growls from under her chair indicated the presence of the woolly dog. She talked with confounding culture of the books that rose all round her to the ceiling; her evening dress was accomplished by means of an additional white shawl, rather dirtier than its congeners; as I took her into dinner she quoted Virgil to me, and in the same breath screeched an objurgation at a being whose matted head rose suddenly into view from behind an ancient Chinese screen, as I have seen the head of a Zulu woman peer over a bush.

Dinner was as incongruous as everything else. Detestable soup in a splendid old silver tureen that was nearly as dark in hue as Robinson Crusoe's thumb; a perfect salmon, perfectly cooked, on a chipped kitchen dish; such cut glass as is not easy to find nowadays; sherry that, as Flurry subsequently remarked, would burn the shell off an egg; and a bottle of port, draped in immemorial cobwebs, wan with age, and probably priceless. Throughout the vicissitudes of the meal Mrs Knox's conversation flowed on undismayed, directed sometimes at me – she had installed me in the position of friend of her youth – and talked to me as if I were my own grandfather – sometimes at Crusoe, with whom she had several heated arguments, and sometimes she would make a statement of remarkable frankness on the subject of her horse-farming affairs to Flurry, who, very much on his best behaviour, agreed with all she said, and risked no original remark. As I listened to them both, I remembered with infinite amusement how he had told me once that a pet name she had for him was 'Tony Lumpkin', and no one but herself knew what she meant by it. It seemed strange that she made no allusion to Trinket's colt or to Flurry's birthday, but mindful of my instructions, I held my peace.

As, at about half past eight, we drove away in the moonlight, Flurry congratulated me solemnly on my success with his grandmother. He was good enough to tell me that she would marry me tomorrow if I asked her, and he wished I would, even if it was only to see what a nice grandson he'd be for me. A sympathetic giggle behind me told me that Michael, on the back seat, had heard and relished the jest.

We had left the gates of Aussolas about half a mile behind when, at the corner of the by-road, Flurry pulled up. A short

squat figure rose from the black shadow of a furze bush and
came out in the moonlight, swinging its arms like a cabman
and cursing audibly.

'Oh, murdher, oh, murdher, Misther Flurry! What kept ye
at all? 'Twould perish the crows to be waiting here the way I
am these two hours – '

'Ah, shut your mouth, Slipper!' said Flurry, who, to my
surprise, had turned back the rug and was taking off his
driving coat. 'I couldn't help it. Come on, Yeates, we've got to
get out here.'

'What for?' I asked, in not unnatural bewilderment.

'It's all right. I'll tell you as we go along,' replied my companion, who was already turning to follow Slipper by the by-
road. 'Take the trap on, Michael, and wait at the River's
Cross.' He waited for me to come up with him, and then put
his hand on my arm. 'You see, Major, this is the way it is. My
grandmother's given me that colt right enough, but if I waited
for her to send him over to me I'd never see a hair of his tail.
So I just thought that as we were over here we might as well
take him back with us, and maybe you'll give us a help with
him; he'll not be altogether too handy for a first go off.'

I was staggered. An infant in arms could scarcely have
failed to discern the fishiness of the transaction, and I begged
Mr Knox not to put himself to this trouble on my account, as I
had no doubt I could find a horse for my friend elsewhere. Mr
Knox assured me that it was no trouble at all, quite the contrary, and that, since his grandmother had given him the colt,
he saw no reason why he should not take him when he wanted him; also, that if I didn't want him he'd be glad enough to
keep him himself; and finally, that I wasn't the chap to go back
on a friend, but I was welcome to drive back to Shreelane with
Michael this minute if I liked.

Of course I yielded in the end. I told Flurry I should lose
my job over the business, and he said I could then marry his
grandmother, and the discussion was abruptly closed by the
necessity of following Slipper over a locked five-barred gate.

Our pioneer took us over about half a mile of country,
knocking down stone gaps where practicable and scrambling
over tall banks in the deceptive moonlight. We found our-

selves at length in a field with a shed in one corner of it; in a dim group of farm buildings a little way off a light was shining.

'Wait here,' said Flurry to me in a whisper; 'the less noise, the better. It's an open shed, and we'll just slip in and coax him out.'

Slipper unwound from his waist a halter, and my colleagues glided like spectres into the shadow of the shed, leaving me to meditate on my duties as Resident Magistrate, and on the questions that would be asked in the House by our local member when Slipper had given away the adventure in his cups.

In less than a minute three shadows emerged from the shed, where two had gone in. They had got the colt.

'He came out as quiet as a calf when he winded the sugar,' said Flurry; 'it was well for me I filled my pockets from grandmamma's sugar basin.'

He and Slipper had a rope from each side of the colt's head; they took him quickly across a field towards the gate. The colt stepped daintily between them over the moonlit grass; he snorted occasionally, but appeared on the whole amenable.

The trouble began later, and was due, as trouble often is, to the beguilements of a short cut. Against the maturer judgment of Slipper, Flurry insisted on following a route that he assured us he knew as well as his own pocket, and the consequence was that in about five minutes I found myself standing on top of a bank hanging on to a rope, on the other end of which the colt dangled and danced, while Flurry, with the other rope, lay prone in the ditch, and Slipper administered to the bewildered colt's hind quarters such chastisement as could be ventured on.

I have no space to narrate in detail the atrocious difficulties and disasters of the short cut. How the colt set to work to buck, and went away across a field, dragging the faithful Slipper, literally *ventre à terre*, after him, while I picked myself in ignominy out of a briar patch, and Flurry cursed himself black in the face. How we were attacked by ferocious cur dogs, and I lost my eye-glass; and how, as we neared the

River's Cross, Flurry espied the police patrol on the road, and we all hid behind a rick of turf while I realised in fullness what an exceptional ass I was, to have been beguiled into an enterprise that involved hiding with Slipper from the Royal Irish Constabulary.

Let it suffice to say that Trinket's infernal offspring was finally handed over on the high road to Michael and Slipper, and Flurry drove me home in a state of mental and physical overthrow.

I saw nothing of my friend Mr Knox for the next couple of days, by the end of which time I had worked up a high polish on my misgivings, and had determined to tell him that under no circumstances would I have anything to say to his grandmother's birthday present. It was like my usual luck that, instead of writing a note to this effect, I thought it would be good for my liver to walk across the hills to Tory Cottage and tell Flurry so in person.

It was a bright, blustery morning, after a muggy day. The feeling of spring was in the air, the daffodils were already in bud, and crocuses showed purple in the grass on either side of the avenue. It was only a couple of miles to Tory Cottage by the way across the hills; I walked fast, and it was barely twelve o'clock when I saw its pink walls and clumps of evergreens below me. As I looked down at it the chiming of Flurry's hounds in the kennels came to me on the wind; I stood still to listen, and could almost have sworn that I was hearing again the clash of Magdalen bells, hard at work on May morning.

The path that I was following led downwards through a larch plantation to Flurry's back gate. Hot wafts from some hideous cauldron at the other side of a wall apprised me of the vicinity of the kennels and their cuisine, and the fir-trees round were hung with gruesome and unknown joints. I thanked heaven that I was not a master of hounds, and passed on as quickly as might be to the hall door.

I rang two or three times without response; then the door opened a couple of inches and was instantly slammed in my face. I heard the hurried paddling of bare feet on oil-cloth, and a voice, 'Hurry, Bridgie, hurry! There's quality at the door!'

Bridgie, holding a dirty cap on with one hand, presently

arrived and informed me that she believed Mr Knox was out about the place. She seemed perturbed, and she cast scared glances down the drive while speaking to me.

I knew enough of Flurry's habits to shape a tolerably direct course for his whereabouts. He was, as I had expected, in the training paddock, a field behind the stable yard, in which he had put up practice jumps for his horses. It was a good-sized field with clumps of furze in it, and Flurry was standing near one of these with his hands in his pockets, singularly unoccupied. I supposed that he was prospecting for a place to put up another jump. He did not see me coming, and turned with a start as I spoke to him. There was a queer expression of mingled guilt and what I can only describe as divilment in his grey eyes as he greeted me. In my dealings with Flurry Knox, I have since formed the habit of sitting tight, in a general way, when I see that expression.

'Well, who's coming next, I wonder!' he said, as he shook hands with me. 'It's not ten minutes since I had two of your d----d peelers here searching the whole place for my grandmother's colt!'

'What!' I exclaimed, feeling cold all down my back. 'Do you mean the police have got hold of it?'

'They haven't got hold of the colt anyway,' said Flurry, looking sideways at me from under the peak of his cap, with the glint of the sun in his eye. 'I got word in time before they came.'

'What do you mean?' I demanded. 'Where is he? For heaven's sake don't tell me you've sent the brute over to my place!'

'It's a good job for you I didn't,' replied Flurry, 'as the police are on their way to Shreelane this minute to consult you about it. You!' He gave utterance to one of his short diabolical fits of laughter. 'He's where they'll not find him, anyhow. Ho! Ho! It's the funniest hand I ever played!'

'Oh yes, it's devilish funny, I've no doubt,' I retorted, beginning to lose my temper, as is the manner of many people when they are frightened; 'but I give you fair warning that if Mrs Knox asks me any question about it, I shall tell her the whole story.'

'All right,' responded Flurry; 'and when you do, don't forget to tell her how you flogged the colt out on to the road over her own bounds ditch.'

'Very well,' I said hotly, 'I may as well go home and send in my papers. They'll break me over this – '

'Ah, hold on, Major,' said Flurry soothingly, 'it'll be all right. No one knows anything. It's only on spec the old lady sent the bobbies here. If you'll keep quiet it'll all blow over.'

'I don't care,' I said, struggling hopelessly in the toils; 'if I meet your grandmother, and she asks me about it, I shall tell her all I know.'

'Please God you'll not meet her! After all, it's not once in a blue moon that she – ' began Flurry. Even as he said the words his face changed. 'Holy fly!' he ejaculated. 'Isn't that her dog coming into the field? Look at her bonnet over the wall! Hide, hide for your life!' He caught me by the shoulder and shoved me down among the furze bushes before I realised what had happened.

'Get in here! I'll talk to her.'

I may as well confess that at the mere sight of Mrs Knox's purple bonnet my heart had turned to water. In that moment I knew what it would be like to tell her how I, having eaten her salmon, and capped her quotations, and drunk her best port, had gone forth and helped to steal her horse. I abandoned my dignity, my sense of honour; I took the furze prickles to my breast and wallowed in them.

Mrs Knox had advanced with vengeful speed; already she was in high altercation with Flurry at no great distance from where I lay; varying sounds of battle reached me, and I gathered that Flurry was not – to put it mildly – shrinking from that economy of truth that the situation required.

'Is it that curby, long-backed brute? You promised him to me long ago, but I wouldn't be bothered with him!'

The old lady uttered a laugh of shrill derision. 'Is it likely I'd promise you my best colt? And still more, is it likely that you'd refuse if I did?'

'Very well, ma'am.' Flurry's voice was admirably indignant. 'Then I suppose I'm a liar and a thief.'

'I'd be more obliged to you for the information if I hadn't

known it before,' responded his grandmother with lightning speed; 'If you swore to me on a stack of Bibles you knew nothing about my colt, I wouldn't believe you! I shall go straight to Major Yeates and ask his advice. I believe him to be a gentleman, in spite of the company he keeps!'

I writhed deeper into the furze bushes, and thereby discovered a sandy rabbit run, along which I crawled, with my cap well over my eyes, and the furze needles stabbing me through my stockings. The ground shelved a little, promising profounder concealment, but the bushes were very thick, and I laid hold of the bare stem of one to help my progress. It lifted out of the ground in my hand, revealing a freshly cut stump. Something snorted, not a yard away; I glared through the opening, and was confronted by the long, horrified face of Mrs Knox's colt, mysteriously on a level with my own.

Even without the white diamond on his forehead I should have divined the truth; but how in the name of wonder had Flurry persuaded him to couch like a woodcock in the heart of a furze brake? For a full minute I lay as still as death for fear of frightening him, while the voices of Flurry and his grandmother raged on alarmingly close to me. The colt snorted, and blew long breaths through his wide nostrils, but he did not move. I crawled an inch or two nearer, and after a few seconds of cautious peering I grasped the position. They had buried him.

A small sandpit among the furze had been utilised as a grave; they had filled him up to his withers with sand, and a few furze bushes, artistically disposed around the pit, had done the rest. As the depth of Flurry's guile was revealed, laughter came upon me like a flood; I gurgled and shook apoplectically, and the colt gazed at me with serious surprise, until a sudden outburst of barking close to my elbow administered a fresh shock to my tottering nerves.

Mrs Knox's woolly dog had tracked me into the furze, and was now baying at the colt and me with mingled terror and indignation. I addressed him in a whisper, with perfidious endearments, advancing a crafty hand towards him the while, made a snatch for the back of his neck, missed it badly, and got him by the ragged fleece of his hindquarters as he tried to flee. If I had flayed him alive, he could hardly have uttered a more deafening series of yells, but, like a fool, instead of letting him go, I dragged him towards me, and tried to stifle the noise by holding his muzzle. The tussle lasted engrossingly for a few seconds, and then the climax of the nightmare arrived.

Mrs Knox's voice, close behind me, said, 'Let go my dog this instant, sir! Who are you – ?'

Her voice faded away, and I knew that she also had seen the colt's head.

I positively felt sorry for her. At her age there was no knowing what effect the shock might have on her. I scrambled to my feet and confronted her.

'Major Yeates!' she said. There was a deathly pause. 'Will you kindly tell me,' said Mrs Knox slowly, 'am I in Bedlam, or are you? And what is that?'

She pointed to the colt, and that unfortunate animal, recognising the voice of his mistress, uttered a hoarse and lamentable whinny. Mrs Knox felt around her for support, found only furze prickles, gazed speechlessly at me, and then, to her eternal honour, fell into wild cackles of laughter.

So, I may say, did Flurry and I. I embarked on my explanation and broke down; Flurry followed suit and broke down too. Overwhelming laughter held us all three, disintegrating into our very souls. Mrs Knox pulled herself together first.

'I acquit you, Major Yeates, I acquit you, though appearances are against you. It's clear enough to me you've fallen among thieves.' She stopped and glowered at Flurry. Her purple bonnet was over one eye. 'I'll thank you, sir,' she said, 'to dig out that horse before I leave this place. And when you've dug him out, you may keep him. I'll be no receiver of stolen goods!'

She broke off and shook her fist at him. 'Upon my conscience, Tony, I'd give a guinea to have thought of it myself!'

A Matter of Opinion

by Eamon Kelly

A SCHOLAR AND A poet were debating. The scholar was a big lump of a man of a very serious turn of mind. The poet was the direct opposite and thin, the Lord save us, if he turned sideways he'd be marked absent. They were debating how long it was since the first Irishman set foot in America. Weren't they short taken for a topic of conversation! The scholar said, 'I suppose that honour will have to go to St Brendan the Sailor. Wasn't it he discovered America, though this fact is not too widely known? St Brendan kept his mouth shut about it.'

'Maybe,' says the poet, 'the world might be a happier place today if the other man did the same thing.'

The scholar never smiled, so the poet said, 'How long ago is it now since St Brendan set foot in America?'

'Well,' says the scholar, 'I think I can work that out.' He settled himself in a chair and then he said with great weight, 'St Brendan was born near Fenit in the County Kerry in the year 532 – that's AD of course – and after a lifetime spent sailing the high seas, spreading the good word, he died in Anach Chuain on the shores of Lough Corrib, where he built that big monastery, in the year 580. Now if we take it that the bulk of St Brendan's exploring was done in his prime, I would say that it is every day of fourteen hundred years since the first Irishman set foot in America.'

'Is that all you know!' says the poet. 'Irishmen were going to America before that.'

'Can you prove it?' says the scholar.

'To be sure I can,' says the poet.' When my great-grand-uncle was going to America before the famine – in a sailing vessel he was – and a couple of hundred miles out from the coast of Clare what happened this evening but the ship was becalmed. The captain threw out the anchor and they all went to bed for the night. What did they want up for?

'Came the morning and there was a nice breeze blowing. The captain drew in the anchor and do you know what was tied on to it? The wheel of a horse car.'

'And what does that prove?' says the scholar.

'It proves,' says the poet, 'that Irish people were going to America by road before the flood!'

THE LOOKING GLASS

by Eamon Kelly

'TIS ALWAYS A MYSTERY to me how the women got on before the looking glass was invented, or indeed the men if it went to that; they are often enough in front of it. Well, the looking glass was invented and there was this man ignorant of the fact. He was living in an out-of-the-way place.

There was an excursion and he availed himself of the cheap fare to travel out, and when he landed in the city he went down the main street and into this shop where he saw a heap of shiny things on the counter. Little oblongs they were, no bigger than a small fag box. He took up one and held it up that way in front of his face.

'Will you look at that,' says he 'a picture of my father wherever they got it.'

Turning to the girl inside the counter, he said, 'What are these selling for?'

She told him. Ah, 'twas only a trifle, so he bought the looking glass and put it in his inside pocket and brought it home. Every opportunity he got he'd take it out to admire what he thought was a picture of his father – a man he had great respect for and who was dead this long time. But he was always very careful not to let the wife see him, for indeed she didn't have the same respect for the father-in-law. Which of 'em have!

As we all know, very little goes unknown to the women. And she saw him and she wondered greatly what was taking him to the pocket and what it was he was admiring. Curiosity was killing her. Finally her chance came. What happened this day but a neighbour's chimney to go on fire. Her husband, when he heard all the *hilaboherk,* dashed out and in the excitement he forgot his coat. Well, his back was hardly turned when his wife went to his pocket and took out the looking glass and held it in front of her face.

'Well,' says she, 'could you be up to him! or who is this old hairpin? And, indeed, wherever he met her, she's no great shakes. I tell you,' says she, 'if that is the attraction that's drawing him away to the city, I'll soon put a halt to his gallop!'

So she put the looking glass back in his pocket and geared herself for battle. And we all know what women in a like situation can be. Her husband came in after doing the good turn for the neighbour. She said what was on her mind. Was he getting tired of her? He denied it.

'And what are you doing so,' she said, 'with this other Dolly Varden inside in your pocket?'

Now that the cat was out of the bag, he thought it would be just as well to admit what was in his pocket. So he said, 'That's only a picture of my father.'

And do you think did she believe him? She did not. 'You'll hear more of this,' she said, putting on her coat and bonnet and going to the priest's house. That was the court of appeal at the time.

Well, the parish priest when he heard her story, you could knock him down with a feather. Her husband was well known to him. A nice, quiet, sober, natural, pious, devout man, exactly what Fr John said.

'God help your head, Father,' says she; 'he has me fooled up to the ball of my eye, and what's more he has a picture of this strange woman in his pocket pretending 'tis his father.'

'Oh, in that case,' says Fr John, 'I'll have to go to the house and reprimand him.' And of course Fr John was right. Wouldn't this be a nice headline to be giving his congregation!

Away to the house went the two, Fr John and the woman and, lifting the latch, the parish priest said:

'Here now, my good man, this is gone far enough. Hand me out the picture of that strange woman you have in your pocket.'

Well, the poor man, he was praying for the ground to open and swallow him, he was so ashamed and upset at the turn things were taking. He went to his coat pocket and took out the looking glass and gave it to the parish priest. Fr John put it up in front of his face, and when he saw who was staring out at him, he had to smile and, turning to the man's wife, he said, 'No doubt in life but you'd want to have your eyes examined. Isn't that the parish priest that was here before me!'

The Umbrella

by Eamon Kelly

ONCE EVERY FIVE YEARS the people of this townland collect into Larry's house and the priest comes and hears confessions and says Mass there.

This function is called the station. It is an old custom going back to the penal times when people of our way of thinking had to worship in holes and corners. Twice a year the station would take place – in the spring and in the harvest. It was a movable feast, going to a different house each time, and as there are ten houses in our townland, once every five years it came to Larry's turn to take the station. 'Often enough,' Larry used to say, 'if you look at it from the point of view of expense!' Like many another good Christian, he was a man of limited resources, and the house had to be painted inside and out, provisions had to be laid in, as well as a little light refreshment for the people. All of which, Larry used to say, did not take place unknown to his pocket.

Well, to get on with the story, it so happened one year that the station was published for Larry. I don't remember this too well myself. My father I heard talking about it, and what kept it so fresh in his memory was something comical that took place the morning of the station. It seems the priest we had here at the time was a trifle hasty, a little impatient and stern of demeanour. Signs on it, innocent people were peppering afraid of him. Although to go to his house, I was told, you couldn't meet a nicer man. Jeremiah Horgan that was telling me. Jeremiah was at the house for a letter of freedom. He was marrying some bird from an outside community. He got the letter – as things turned out, he'd be better off if he didn't.

Come the morning of the station and all the neighbours were waiting in Larry's yard for Fr John. The morning turned out very wet, but of course country people don't mind the rain, they say it never melted anyone. With that a son of Johnny Dan Tadhgeen's put his head around the corner of the house and said, 'He's coming!' the yard emptied itself into the kitchen, leaving only Larry to welcome Fr John, and Larry'd rather any other job – he'd rather be draining the Dead Sea with a silver spoon – for he was a very shy, distant sort of individual. He hadn't long to wait. Fr John came riding into the yard on a saddle horse, holding over his head a black round roof on top of a walking cane.

This strange object left poor Larry speechless, for it was the first umbrella that was seen in this townland. He didn't say 'Good morning', or 'Good day' or 'It was good of you to come', only took the priest's horse and put him in the stable. Fr John made off into the kitchen, and when those inside saw the doorway darkening, every man turned his back, making himself small behind his neighbour in case any awkward question should be put to him.

When they turned around again, Fr John had opened the umbrella at the bottom of the kitchen so as that the rain'd be running off it and that it'd be nice and dry when he'd be going home bye 'n' bye, that is when confessions'd be heard Mass'd be said, breakfast'd be ate and dues'd be collected.

The morning wore on and all these things came to pass and the grace of God, glory be to Him, was in the house and Fr John was in the room having his breakfast.

The women were up and down on him, taking the legs off one another with excitement, and Larry's wife said, and her face as red as a coal of fire, 'If you saw the look he gave me when he took the top off the egg!'

'Were they too done?' says Cáit.

'Bullets, girl! And I wouldn't mind, but I told that daughter of mine not to take her eyes off the eggs. But there you are – the morning you'd want a thing to go right for you, that's the morning everything'd break the melt in you.'

The men were in the kitchen around the umbrella the same as if it was a German bomber. And they were saying that for such a simple thing, wasn't it a great wonder someone didn't think of it long 'go. And how handy it would be, they said, to prop it over the mouth of the barrel in the yard a wet day where you'd have a goose hatching. On the heel of that remark Fr John came up from the room. They all backed toward the fire.

'Morning men,' he said. 'What's the day doing?'

''Tis brightening, Father,' says John Cronin, a forward class of a man anyway.

'I'll be going,' he said. 'There's many the thing I could be doing.'

'Good morning, Father,' they all said, and said it very loud and with great relief, for they knew that the bottle wouldn't be opened until he was gone.

Larry took the priest's horse from the stable and conveyed Fr John down the passageway to the main road. They were nearly halfway down when Fr John thought of his umbrella. 'Run up to the house,' he said to Larry, 'and bring me out my parasol.'

He didn't have to say this secondly. Larry ran up to the house and into the kitchen breathless. He took the umbrella by the leg, 'twas open, and brought it after him to the door, but it wouldn't go out. He came inside it and tried to shove it out before him, but the devil a out it'd go. He looked at those in the kitchen and they looked at him and they had pity for him. He took the door off the hinges – that'd give him an extra inch – but the umbrella wouldn't go out. Little beads of perspiration began to stand out on his forehead at the thought of Fr John waiting in the passageway. He began muttering to himself, saying, 'If it came in, it must go out.'

Well, there was a small man there and, wanting to be of

help, he said, 'I wonder would it be any value if we kicked out the two sides of the door frame.' The two sides of the frame were driven out in the yard, but the umbrella remained inside. 'Well,' says Larry, 'there's nothing for it now only knock down the wall.' A sledge hammer was procured and when Father John heard all the pounding, he doubled back to the house. And when he saw what was happening, 'twas as good as a tonic to him. He roared out laughing. 'What are you at?' says he. 'Well, do you know now, Father,' says Larry, 'I think myself that if I got the cornerstone there down, the mushroom'd sail out – no trouble.'

'Move into the kitchen from me,' says he. They did. Fr John took the umbrella by the leg – 'twas open, as I said – and brought it to the door in front of him. He was a fierce big man, God bless him, overcoat and all on a wet day, and they couldn't see what was happening. When he came to the door, like lightening he shut the umbrella and opened it again outside and walked out the yard holding it over his head, leaving them there spellbound.

When he was gone, Larry turned to his neighbours and said, 'Say what ye like, *they* have the power!'

WAY OF WOMEN

by Paul Jones

'I HEAR YOUR DAUGHTER'S all packed up to go on her holidays,' said Hennessey.

'She is,' said Hogan.

'That's more than you and I were ever able to do when we were her age,' said Hennessey.

'It is,' said Hogan.

'Extraordinary how the years roll by!' said Hennessey. 'It seems only yesterday when she was climbing over the wall in a little pink frock down on top of my rhubarb to get her ball back, and now I suppose she's a young lady with a half-pitying smile when old fogeys like you and I express an opinion about anything.'

'She is,' said Hogan, 'and maybe she's right.'

'Maybe she is,' said Hennessey. 'I'll say this for her. She's a nice girl and a great credit to her mother. Where's she going?'

'To Ballybunion,' said Hogan. 'I hope it's a nice place. She deserves a holiday after twelve months in a solicitor's office. What kind of a place is it?'

'Listen, Hogan,' said Hennessey. 'It doesn't matter what

sort of a place it is. Would you like me to tell you eternal truth about girls and holidays?'

'I would,' said Hogan.

'When a girl,' said Hennessey, 'says that such and such a place is a lovely place for a holiday, all she means is that she met a nice young fellow there, or two or three nice young fellows, and preferably, nice young fellows with a car. It doesn't matter if the place itself is devoid of scenic or historic or any other attraction and is as flat as the back of me hand. I don't know what sort of a place Ballybunion is, but I'll tell you this. If, two days after she arrives there, you get a postcard of a hunk of the local landscape with 'Having a lovely time here, Love, Peggy' scrawled on it, and five pence to pay because she's forgotten the stamp, you'll know she's met one already. And if she comes home and says, 'Ballybunion's a lovely place for a holiday!' all that'll mean will be that she'll be staying in at night waiting for the telephone to ring and getting up early in the morning to see if there's a letter.'

Ireland's Different to England – See?

by Patrick Campbell

THE SUMMER WAS IN progress one morning last year in the village of Rooskey, on the River Shannon, in Co. Longford. The rain was descending vertically on the deck of a cabin-cruiser in which, at the early hour of 9.45, I was taking breakfast in bed.

All at once, unexpected as the roaring of a lion, an English accent established itself on the jetty. 'I say!' it cried. 'I say, is anyone there?'

We love strangers in Ireland. You never know what they're going to be like. With high expectation I drew back the six inches of chintz concealing the porthole, and there he was – a splendid specimen of English holiday male, fully grown with all his distinguishing marks ablaze.

He wore, in the downpour, his wife's transparent plastic mackintosh, and a transparent pixie hood. Under the mackintosh I could see a striped Shaftesbury-Avenue-Italian jersey and a pair of white shorts. On his feet he wore yellow socks and new, brown leather sandals. 'I say,' he called. 'I say, is anyone there?'

I let him know, through the porthole, that a fellow human was present, while warning him that it was practically the middle of the night. 'Or perhaps,' I said, 'you're still on the way to bed.' There had been, the previous evening, a Grand Gala Ball in aid of the church in a fancy *palais* called Dreamland on the other side of the river, which had terminated round about 4 a.m. – a normal social occasion in Irish rural life.

He knelt down on the jetty, presenting me with a close-up through the frame of the porthole of the pixie hood, and a pale, anxious face. 'Hello, there,' he said. 'Actually, I was looking for some milk.' He held up a small, plastic jug, making his mission clear. The rain poured into it as though from a tap.

We love strangers in Ireland. It's the last place left in the British Isles where you'll find a deeply appreciative audience if you want to talk about yourself. I invited him to fill in the details of how he came to be standing on Tony Fallon's jetty at the stark hour of 9.45, wearing a pixie hood and carrying a plastic jug.

He provided some facts. He was cruising with his wife and family, and had made an early start, to cover twenty miles before breakfast, as they had only a week and wished to see as much of the Shannon as possible in this short space of time. His wife and children were very hungry, but they couldn't start breakfast until they had some milk. He gestured with the jug toward Tony Fallon's.

'The shop,' he said, 'doesn't seem to be open.'

It's always a pleasure to us in Ireland to give information to a stranger, because he can scarcely ever believe his ears.

'Owing to the licensing laws,' I said, 'the shop doesn't open until the legal hour of 10.30, but when it does, you'll be able to buy not only a bottle of milk but also a packet of aspirin, a bar of cut-plug, a tin of peaches, a rat-trap, a screwdriver, half a pound of streaky bacon, a length of clothes-line, a jar of honey, a fishing rod, a morning paper, and a bottle of stout with which to wash it down. What's more, Tony's got a piano in the back lounge, so that while waiting you'll be able to play and sing. In addition, you'll be able to deal in all these commodities and pleasures for thirteen hours without a break, because the place doesn't shut until 11.30 tonight.'

'I see,' he said, though the concept was obviously new to him. 'I suppose,' he suggested after a moment, 'there isn't a sort of dairy where I could just buy a bottle of milk?'

'There's one on the other side of the river,' I told him, 'but you'd have to walk nearly half a mile in the rain, and then it mightn't be open. The butcher, for instance, only comes to Rooskey once a week, and then he chops up carcasses in a rented sitting-room, with floral paper on the walls. Ireland's different to England, you see. The individual runs the country here, not the country the individual, and no individuals are up and about yet, so if I were you, I'd go back to bed until they get the place aired.'

Ireland is beautiful to look at, the beauty of desolation. Long, white roads, the only traveller for miles an old woman in a black shawl on a donkey cart. The light is ever changing on the distant mountains, as the tall clouds sail in from the Atlantic. There is complete silence. A curlew pipes suddenly, but there is nothing else. A shaft of sunlight turns the bog to gold. Then the clouds darken again over the purple hills and the soft rain comes down and everything turns to pearly grey and luminous green. Machines and houses, brick walls and concrete and barbed wire died out before they got here. It's the uttermost, empty edge of Europe, the silent prehistoric land of Hy Brazil. It makes a haunting, quite unforgettable impression even on jolly, orange-sucking coach-parties from Manchester, Scunthorpe and Hull, so that, once bitten by it, they always come back, to recapture the strange feeling of being one's own man in a lost and dreamlike world, where there's no need to do anything in a hurry because you can be perfectly certain that no one else will be there to do it for you or with you ... until we've got the place aired, and then there's a fair chance there'll be no need to do it at all.

It's a slowing down of the tempo that the English find difficult to get in step with at first, and even when they find the beat, they're never quite happy, being a people over-concerned with immediate practicalities, but on the other hand it provides them with an experience they never forget.

Take, for instance, the case of this milk-seeking Englishman. I went over to Tony Fallon's pub at about eleven o'clock, having a number of urgent commissions on my mind, to find him, still in his pixie hood and transparent mac, stamping up and down the light hardware and tinned comestibles department of the shop, and still calling, though on a more strained note than before, 'I say, there – I say!' He had his plastic jug with him, but it was empty.

He was glad to see me. 'I say,' he said, 'there seems to be no one here. A girl opened the shop at half past ten, but she's disappeared.'

I was able to clarify the position. 'Our genial host,' I said, 'Mr Tony Fallon, is heir apparent to the resident undertaker, so he's gone to a funeral to polish up his technique with the ropes that go round the coffin. The beautiful girl who opened the door is his sister Patty, and she is now putting ten gallons of petrol into a lorry across the road, because Tony Fallon owns the filling station as well. She may be there for some time because the lorry driver has just arrived from Belturbet and she has a natural desire to know what's going on in a metropolis of that size. I don't know where Mrs Fallon is, but she's got two small children and is probably attending to them. Have a bottle of stout.'

'But I haven't had breakfast yet,' he said. 'We've no milk.'

I went into the bar at the back and pulled two bottles of stout, leaving the money in an ashtray. 'But what about breakfast?' he said. 'We want to get provisioned up, and make a start – '

'If you're going downstream,' I said, 'there's no point in leaving now because I'm meeting the lock-keeper here at midday, and giving him a lift. He's seventy-eight, but he's never been in a cabin-cruiser and wants to broaden his mind. He might be here earlier, but that won't help because we've lost a child and can't start without her.'

He became overconcerned with practicalities. 'You've lost a child? Where? How? Have you told the police?'

'The police,' I said, 'are in the back bar. He's having a bottle of stout and reading the paper. The child went into Longford on the nine o'clock bus to buy some comics – she hates boats. She should have been back here by ten, but she didn't arrive, so she's obviously lost.'

He forgot about his milk troubles. 'What are you doing about it?'

'Nothing,' I said. 'She's got plaits and she's wearing leopardskin trousers. Someone in Longford is bound to fall into conversation with such an interesting-looking visitor, and then they'll ring up about her. What I'm really worried about is getting some flexible cable to repair the steering gear, but the police thinks he knows a man in Mohill who might have some, so we're going there as soon as Tony comes back from the funeral with the car. There's one little difficulty about the car. Tony's just sold it, in his function as a garagist, to a man who's coming to collect it, but if he turns up before we leave for Mohill, he can take us there himself.'

He sifted through it, and came up with a matter which he considered affected himself. 'This lock-keeper,' he said. 'Do you mean I can't get through without him? We wanted to start in about ten minutes.'

'You'd better have another bottle of stout,' I said. 'The lock-keeper is coming up from the lock in the new water-bus, because it can't get past here until the lock-keeper opens the swing bridge. He doesn't want to come up on his bicycle because he's going back to the lock with me. But in any case,' I said, 'there's no great hurry because a man's dropping in here on his way to Sligo to show me some new charts of the river, and there's a strong rumour that he broke down last night in Mullingar.'

'I see,' said the Englishman. 'I think,' he said tightly, 'I'd better go and tell my wife.'

It turned out to be a wonderful day, the kind of day you get only in Ireland where past, present and future, and day and night, blend into an endless, whirling dream, into which new characters constantly intrude and stay a while and vanish, unexplained – a dream of comings and goings and long talks with total strangers, of songs and loud laughter, of sudden friendships with people entirely unknown, and everything wrapped in this feeling of timelessness and buoyant, floating ease.

The Englishman, the lock-keeper, the policeman, the postman and I spent a good deal of it in the distant town of Mohill, negotiating for flexible steel cable in perhaps twelve different pubs. When we got back to Rooskey, the lock-keeper opened the swing bridge for the water-bus. We stood on it, while he wound the handle, wondering at the power of machinery. In Tony Fallon's we found that the Englishman's wife and my wife had set off in a speedboat at thirty-five knots for Carrick-on-Shannon on the way to Sligo. Tony had, it seemed, been compelled to make a detour, for business or social reasons, to Longford, where general rumour quickly led him to a child in leopardskin trousers, contentedly browsing in a bookshop, having spent her return fare.

'That,' as I explained to the Englishman, 'is the wonderful thing about Ireland, our passionate interest in life, and in human beings. For twenty miles all up and down the river, people have heard there are two cabin-cruisers in Rooskey, and there's a young one missing, in leopardskin trousers. A man we met in Mohill passed it on to a fella in Drumlish, who met another fella at the crossroads in Ballinalee, so it's a wonder they didn't hear in Longford that a tiger was loose from Dublin Zoo. I bet you,' I said, 'there's fellas as far away as Sligo town itself who have heard there might be a bit of a do tonight in Tony Fallon's, and they're coming here now by way of Galway.'

A car pulled up at the filling station. A head came out of the window. It was a man I hadn't seen for ten years. 'I heard', said he, 'below in Athlone you were up this way. Are you buying?' We brought him inside.

Timelessness and buoyancy and ease. The wives and the man with the speedboat came back, and he played the piano, so they started another gala ball in the back room. A middle-aged and studious American couple came in, Pennsylvania Quakers by persuasion, touring Ireland in search of Celtic crosses. Within a few moments they were absorbed in conversation with a very old farmer whose brother, during the Jimmy Walker administration, had been a policeman in New York. There was a Swedish couple as well, who suddenly materialised from the wind and the rain of the Irish night. You'd have thought the whole world was gathered together.

By 11.30, and closing time, the back room and the bar and the shop were packed so tightly we could only stand, shoulder to shoulder, and sing. And it had really begun twelve hours before with an Englishman in a pixie hood looking for a small jug of milk.

That's what happens in Ireland, where the machines and mass entertainment haven't reached, where every man is his own man and makes the day go by as he wishes.

It's what people come to Ireland for.

IVY DAY IN THE COMMITTEE ROOM

by James Joyce

OLD JACK RAKED THE cinders together with a piece of cardboard and spread them judiciously over the whitening dome of coals. When the dome was thinly covered, his face lapsed into darkness but, as he set himself to fan the fire again, his crouching shadow ascended the opposite wall and his face slowly re-emerged into light. It was an old man's face, very bony and hairy. The moist blue eyes blinked at the fire and the moist mouth fell open at times, munching once or twice mechanically when it closed. When the cinders had caught, he laid the piece of cardboard against the wall, sighed and said:

'That's better now, Mr O'Connor.'

Mr O'Connor, a grey-haired young man, whose face was disfigured by many blotches and pimples, had just brought the tobacco for a cigarette into a shapely cylinder, but when spoken to he undid his handiwork meditatively and after a moment's thought decided to lick the paper.

'Did Mr Tierney say when he'd be back?' he asked in a husky falsetto.

'He didn't say.'

Mr O'Connor put his cigarette into his mouth and began

to search his pockets. He took out a pack of thin pasteboard cards.

'I'll get you a match,' said the old man.

'Never mind, this'll do,' said Mr O'Connor.

He selected one of the cards and read what was printed on it:

MUNICIPAL ELECTIONS
Royal Exchange Ward
Mr Richard J. Tierney, P.L.G., respectfully solicits the
favour of your vote and influence at the coming election
in the Royal Exchange Ward.

Mr O'Connor had been engaged by Tierney's agent to canvass one part of the ward but, as the weather was inclement and his boots let in the wet, he spent a great part of the day sitting by the fire in the Committee Room in Wicklow Street with Jack, the old caretaker. They had been sitting thus since the short day had grown dark. It was 6 October, dismal and cold out of doors.

Mr O'Connor tore a strip off the card and, lighting it, lit his cigarette. As he did so the flame lit up a leaf of dark glossy ivy in the lapel of his coat. The old man watched him attentively and then, taking up the piece of cardboard again, began to fan the fire slowly while his companion smoked.

'Ah, yes,' he said, continuing, 'it's hard to know what way to bring up children. Now, who'd think he'd turn out like that! I sent him to the Christian Brothers and I done what I could for him, and there he goes boozing about. I tried to make him someway decent.'

He replaced the cardboard wearily.

'Only I'm an old man now I'd change his tune for him. I'd take the stick to his back and beat him while I could stand over him – as I done many a time before. The mother, you know, she cocks him up with this and that ...'

'That's what ruins children,' said Mr O'Connor.

'To be sure it is,' said the old man. 'And little thanks you get for it, only impudence. He takes th'upper hand of me whenever he sees I've a sup taken. What's the world coming to when sons speak that way to their fathers?'

'What age is he? said Mr O'Connor.

'Nineteen,' said the old man.

'Why don't you put him to something?'

'Sure, amn't I never done at the drunken bowsy ever since he left school? "I won't keep you," I says. "You must get a job for yourself." But, sure, it's worse whenever he gets a job; he drinks it all.'

Mr O'Connor shook his head in sympathy, and the old man fell silent, gazing into the fire. Someone opened the door of the room and called out:

'Hello! Is this a Freemason's meeting?'

'Who's that ?' said the old man.

'What are you doing in the dark?' asked a voice.

'Is that you, Hynes?' asked Mr O'Connor.

'Yes. What are you doing in the dark?' said Mr Hynes, advancing into the light of the fire.

He was a tall, slender young man with a light brown moustache. Imminent little drops of rain hung at the brim of his hat and the collar of his jacket-coat was turned up.

'Well, Matt,' he said to Mr O'Connor, 'how goes it?'

Mr O'Connor shook his head. The old man left the hearth, and after stumbling about the room returned with two candlesticks which he thrust one after the other into the fire and carried to the table. A denuded room came into view and the fire lost all its cheerful colour. The walls of the room were bare except for a copy of an election address. In the middle of the room was a small table on which papers were heaped.

Mr Hynes leaned against the mantelpiece and asked:

'Has he paid you yet?'

'Not yet,' said Mr O'Connor. 'I hope to God he'll not leave us in the lurch tonight.'

Mr Hynes laughed.

'Oh, he'll pay you. Never fear,' he said.

'I hope he'll look smart about it if he means business,' said Mr O'Connor.

'What do you think, Jack?' said Mr Hynes satirically to the old man.

The old man returned to his seat by the fire, saying:

'It isn't but he has it, anyway. Not like the other tinker.'

'What other tinker?' said Mr Hynes.

'Colgan,' said the old man scornfully.

'Is it because Colgan's a working-man you say that? What's the difference between a good honest bricklayer and a publican – eh? Hasn't the working-man as good a right to be in the Corporation as anyone else – ay, and a better right than those shoneens that are always hat in hand before any fellow with a handle to his name? Isn't that, so, Matt?' said Mr Hynes, addressing Mr O'Connor.

'I think you're right,' said Mr O'Connor.

'Our man is a plain honest man with no hunker-sliding about him. He goes in to represent the labour classes. This fellow you're working for only wants to get some job or other.'

'Of course, the working classes should be represented,' said the old man.

'The working-man,' said Mr Hynes, 'gets all kicks and no halfpence. But it's labour produces everything. The working-man is not going to drag the honour of Dublin in the mud to please a German monarch.'

'How's that?' said the old man.

'Don't you know they want to present an address of welcome to Edward Rex if he comes here next year? What do we want kowtowing to a foreign king?'

'Our man won't vote for the address,' said Mr O'Connor. 'Anyway, I wish he'd turn up with the spondulics.'

The three men fell silent. The old man began to rake more cinders together. Mr Hynes took off his hat, shook it and then turned down the collar of his coat, displaying, as he did so, an ivy leaf in the lapel.

'If this man was alive,' he said, pointing to the leaf, 'we'd have no talk of an address of welcome.'

'That's true,' said Mr O'Connor.

'Musha, God be with them times!' said the old man. 'There was some life in it then.'

The room was silent again. Then a bustling little man with a snuffling nose and very cold ears pushed in the door. He walked over quickly to the fire, rubbing his hands as if he intended to produce a spark from them.

'No money, boys,' he said.

'Sit down here, Mr Henchy,' said the old man, offering him his chair.

'Oh, don't stir, Jack; don't stir,' said Mr Henchy.

He nodded curtly to Mr Hynes and sat down on the chair which the old man vacated.

'Did you serve Aungier Street?' he asked Mr O'Connor.

'Yes,' said Mr O'Connor, beginning to search his pockets for memoranda.

'Did you call on Grimes?'

'I did.'

'Well? How does he stand?'

'He wouldn't promise. He said: "I won't tell anyone what way I'm going to vote." But I think he'll be all right.'

'Why so?'

'He asked me who the nominators were, and I told him. I mentioned Fr Burke's name. I think it'll be all right.'

Mr Henchy began to snuffle and to rub his hands over the fire at a terrific speed. Then he said:

'For the love of God, Jack, bring us a bit of coal. There must be some left.'

The old man went out of the room.

'It's no go,' said Mr Henchy, shaking his head. 'I asked the little shoe-boy, but he said: "Oh, now, Mr Henchy, when I see the work going on properly I won't forget you, you may be sure." Mean little tinker! 'Usha, how could he be anything else?'

'What did I tell you, Matt?' said Mr Hynes. 'Tricky Dicky Tierney.'

'Oh, he's as tricky as they make 'em,' said Mr Henchy. 'He hasn't got those little pigs' eyes for nothing. Blast his soul! Couldn't he pay up like a man instead of: "Oh, now, Mr Henchy, I must speak to Mr Fanning ... I've spent a lot of money." Mean little schoolboy of hell! I suppose he forgets the time his little old father kept the hand-me-down shop in Mary's Lane.'

'But is that a fact?' asked Mr O'Connor.

'God, yes,' said Mr Henchy. 'Did you never hear that? And the men used to go in on Sunday morning before the houses were open to buy a waistcoat or a trousers – moya! But

Tricky Dicky's little old father always had a tricky little black bottle up in a corner. Do you mind now? That's that. That's where he first saw the light.'

The old man returned with a few lumps of coal which he placed here and there on the fire.

'That's a nice how-do-you-do,' said Mr O'Connor. 'How does he expect us to work for him if he won't stump up?'

'I can't help it,' said Mr Henchy. 'I expect to find the bailiffs in the hall when I go home.'

Mr Hynes laughed and, shoving himself away from the mantelpiece with the aid of his shoulders, made ready to leave.

'It'll be all right when King Eddie comes,' he said. 'Well, boys, I'm off for the present. See you later. 'Bye, 'bye.'

He went out of the room slowly. Neither Mr Henchy nor the old man said anything, but, just as the door was closing, Mr O'Connor, who had been staring moodily into the fire, called out suddenly:

''Bye, Joe.'

Mr Henchy waited a few moments and then nodded in the direction of the door.

'Tell me,' he said across the fire, 'what brings our friend in here? What does he want?'

''Usha, poor Joe!' said Mr O'Connor, throwing the end of his cigarette into the fire. 'He's hard up, like the rest of us.'

Mr Henchy snuffled vigorously and spat so copiously that he nearly put out the fire, which uttered a hissing protest.

'To tell you my private and candid opinion,' he said, ' I think he's a man from the other camp. He's a spy of Colgan's, if you ask me. Just go round and try and find out how they're getting on. They won't suspect you. Do you twig?'

'Ah, poor Joe is a decent skin,' said Mr O'Connor.

'His father was a decent, respectable man,' Mr Henchy admitted. 'Poor old Larry Hynes! Many a good turn he did in his day! But I'm greatly afraid our friend is not nineteen carat. Damn it, I understand a fellow being hard up, but what I can't understand is a fellow sponging. Couldn't he have some spark of manhood about him?'

'He doesn't get a warm welcome from me when he

comes,' said the old man. 'Let him work for his own side and not come spying around here.'

'I don't know,' said Mr O'Connor dubiously, as he took out cigarette-papers and tobacco. 'I think Joe Hynes is a straight man. He's a clever chap, too, with the pen. Do you remember that thing he wrote ...?'

'Some of these hillsiders and fenians are a bit too clever, if you ask me,' said Mr Henchy. 'Do you know what my private and candid opinion is about some of those little jokers? I believe half of them are in the pay of the Castle.'

'There's no knowing,' said the old man.

'Oh, but I know it for a fact,' said Mr Henchy. 'They're Castle hacks ... I don't say Hynes ... No, damn it, I think he's a stroke above that ... But there's a certain little nobleman with a cock-eye – you know the patriot I'm alluding to?'

Mr O'Connor nodded.

'There's a lineal descendant of Major Sirr for you if you like! Oh, the heart's blood of a patriot! That's a fellow now that'd sell his country for four pence – ay – and go down on his bended knees and thank the Almighty Christ he had a country to sell.'

There was a knock at the door.

'Come in!' said Mr Henchy.

A person resembling a poor clergyman or a poor actor appeared in the doorway. His black clothes were tightly buttoned on his short body and it was impossible to say whether he wore a clergyman's collar or a layman's, because the collar of his shabby frock coat, the uncovered buttons of which reflected the candlelight, was turned up about his neck. He wore a round hat of hard black felt. His face, shining with raindrops, had the appearance of damp yellow cheese save where two rosy spots indicated the cheekbones. He opened his very long mouth suddenly to express disappointment and at the same time opened wide his very bright blue eyes to express pleasure and surprise.

'Oh, Fr Keon!' said Mr Henchy, jumping up from his chair. 'Is that you? Come in!'

'Oh, no, no, no!' said Fr Keon quickly, pursing his lips as if he were addressing a child.

'Won't you come in and sit down?'

'No, no, no!' said Fr Keon, speaking in a discreet, in-
dulgent, velvety voice. 'Don't let me disturb you now! I'm just
looking for Mr Fanning ...'

'He's round at the Black Eagle,' said Mr Henchy. 'But
won't you come in and sit down a minute?'

'No, no, thank you. It was just a little business matter,'
said Fr Keon. 'Thank you, indeed.'

He retreated from the doorway and Mr Henchy, seizing
one of the candlesticks, went to the door to light him downstairs.

'Oh, don't trouble, I beg!'

'No, but the stairs is so dark.'

'No, no, I can see ... Thank you, indeed.'

'Are you right now?'

'All right, thanks ... Thanks.'

Mr Henchy returned with the candlestick and put it on
the table. He sat down again at the fire. There was silence for a
few moments.

'Tell me, John,' said Mr O'Connor, lighting his cigarette
with another pasteboard card.

'Hm?'

'What is he exactly?'

'Ask me an easier one,' said Mr Henchy.

'Fanning and himself seem to me to be very thick. They're
often in Kavanagh's together. Is he a priest at all?'

'Mmm yes, I believe so ... I think he's what you call a
black sheep. We haven't many of them, thank God! but we
have a few ... He's an unfortunate man of some kind....'

'And how does he knock it out?' asked Mr O'Connor.

'That's another mystery.'

'Is he attached to any chapel or church or institution or –'

'No,' said Mr Henchy, 'I think he's travelling on his own
account ... God forgive me,' he added, 'I thought he was the
dozen of stout.'

'Is there any chance of a drink itself?' asked Mr O'Connor.

'I'm dry, too,' said the old man.

'I asked that little shoe-boy three times,' said Mr Henchy,
'would he send up a dozen of stout. I asked him again now,

but he was leaning on the counter in his shirtsleeves having a deep goster with Alderman Cowley.'

'Why didn't you remind him?' said Mr O'Connor.

'Well, I couldn't go over while he was talking to Alderman Cowley. I just waited till I caught his eye, and said: "About that little matter I was speaking to you about ..." "That'll be all right, Mr H," he said. Yerra, sure the little hop-o'-my-thumb has forgotten all about it.'

'There's some deal on in that quarter,' said Mr O'Connor thoughtfully. 'I saw the three of them hard at it yesterday at Suffolk Street corner.'

'I think I know the little game they're at,' said Mr Henchy. 'You must owe the City Fathers money nowadays if you want to be made Lord Mayor. Then they'll make you a Lord Mayor. By God! I'm thinking seriously of becoming a City Father myself. What do you think? Would I do for the job?'

Mr O'Connor laughed.

'So far as owing money goes ...'

'Driving out of the Mansion House,' said Mr Henchy, 'in all my vermin, with Jack here standing up behind me in a powdered wig – eh?'

'And make me your private secretary, John.'

'Yes. And I'll make Fr Keon my private chaplain. We'll have a family party.'

'Faith, Mr Henchy,' said the old man, 'you'd keep up better style than some of them. I was talking one day to old Keegan, the porter. "And how do you like your new master, Pat?" says I to him. "You haven't much entertaining now," says I. "Entertaining!" says he. "He'd live on the smell of an oil-rag." And do you know what he told me? Now, I declare to God, I didn't believe him.'

'What?' said Mr Henchy and Mr O'Connor.

'He told me: "What do you think of a Lord Mayor of Dublin sending out for a pound of chops for his dinner? How's that for high living?" says he. "Wisha! Wisha!" says I. "A pound of chops," says he, "coming into the Mansion House." "Wisha!" says I. "What kind of people is going at all now?"'

At this point there was a knock at the door, and a boy put in his head.

'What is it?' said the old man.

'From the Black Eagle,' said the boy, walking in sideways and depositing a basket on the floor with a noise of shaken bottles.

The old man helped the boy to transfer the bottles from the basket to the table and counted the full tally. After the transfer the boy put his basket on his arm and asked:

'Any bottles?'

'What bottles?' said the old man.

'Won't you let us drink them first?' said Mr Henchy.

'I was told to ask for the bottles.'

'Come back tomorrow,' said the old man.

'Here, boy!' said Mr Henchy. 'Will you run over to O'Farrell's and ask him to lend us a corkscrew – for Mr Henchy, say. Tell him we won't keep it a minute. Leave the basket there.'

The boy went out and Mr Henchy began to rub his hands cheerfully, saying: 'Ah, well, he's not so bad after all. He's as good as his word, anyhow.'

'There's no tumblers,' said the old man.

'Oh, don't let that trouble you, Jack,' said Mr Henchy. 'Many's the good man before now drank out of the bottle.'

'Anyway, it's better than nothing,' said Mr O'Connor.

'He's not a bad sort,' said Mr Henchy, 'only Fanning has such a loan of him. He means well, you know, in his own tin-pot way.'

The boy came back with the corkscrew. The old man opened three bottles and was handing back the corkscrew when Mr Henchy said to the boy:

'Would you like a drink, boy?'

'If you please, sir,' said the boy.

The old man opened another bottle grudgingly, and handed it to the boy.

'What age are you?' he asked.

'Seventeen,' said the boy.

As the old man said nothing further, the boy took the bottle, said: 'Here's my best respects, sir, to Mr Henchy', drank the contents, put the bottle back on the table and wiped his mouth with his sleeve. Then he took up the corkscrew and went out of the door sideways, muttering some form of salutation.

'That's the way it begins,' said the old man.

'The thin edge of the wedge,' said Mr Henchy.

The old man distributed the three bottles which he had opened and the men drank from them simultaneously. After having drunk, each placed his bottle on the mantelpiece within hand's reach and drew in a long breath of satisfaction.

'Well, I did a good day's work today,' said Mr Henchy, after a pause.

'That so, John?'

'Yes. I got him one or two sure things in Dawson Street, Crofton and myself. Between ourselves, you know, Crofton (he's a decent chap, of course), but he's not worth a damn as a canvasser. He hasn't a word to throw to a dog. He stands and looks at the people while I do the talking.'

Here two men entered the room. One of them was a very fat man, whose blue serge clothes seemed to be in danger of falling from his sloping figure. He had a big face which resembled a young ox's face in expression, staring blue eyes and a grizzled moustache. The other man, who was much younger and frailer, had a thin, clean-shaven face. He wore a very high double collar and a wide-brimmed bowler hat.

'Hello, Crofton!' said Mr Henchy to the fat man. 'Talk of the devil ...'

'Where did the booze come from?' asked the young man. 'Did the cow calve?'

'Oh, of course, Lyons spots the drink first thing!' said Mr O'Connor, laughing.

'Is that the way you chaps canvass,' said Mr Lyons, 'and Crofton and I out in the cold and rain looking for votes?'

'Why, blast your soul,' said Mr Henchy, 'I'd get more votes in five minutes than you two'd get in a week.'

'Open two bottles of stout, Jack,' said Mr O'Connor.

'How can I,' said the old man, 'when there's no corkscrew?'

'Wait now, wait now!' said Mr Henchy, getting up quickly. 'Did you ever see this little trick?'

He took two bottles from the table and, carrying them to

the fire, put them on the hob. Then he sat down again by the fire and took another drink from his bottle. Mr Lyons sat on the edge of the table, pushed his hat towards the nape of his neck and began to swing his legs.

'Which is my bottle?' he asked.

'This lad,' said Mr Henchy.

Mr Crofton sat down on a box and looked fixedly at the other bottle on the hob. He was silent for two reasons. The first reason, sufficient in itself, was that he had nothing to say; the second reason was that he considered his companions beneath him. He had been a canvasser for Wilkins, the Conservative, but when the Conservatives had withdrawn their man and, choosing the lesser of two evils, given their support to the Nationalist candidate, he had been engaged to work for Mr Tierney.

In a few minutes an apologetic 'Pok!' was heard as the cork flew out of Mr Lyons' bottle. Mr Lyons jumped off the table, went to the fire, took his bottle and carried it back to the table.

'I was just telling them, Crofton,' said Mr Henchy, 'that we got a good few votes today.'

'Who did you get?' asked Mr Lyons.

'Well, I got Parkes for one, and I got Atkinson for two, and I got Ward of Dawson Street. Fine old chap he is, too – regular old toff, old Conservative! "But isn't your candidate a Nationalist?" said he. "He's a respectable man," said I. "He's in favour of whatever will benefit this country. He's a big rate-payer," I said. "He has extensive house property in the city and three places of business, and isn't it to his own advantage to keep down the rates? He's a prominent and respected citizen," said I, "and a Poor Law Guardian, and he doesn't belong to any party, good, bad, or indifferent." That's the way to talk to 'em.'

'And what about the address to the King?' said Mr Lyons, after drinking and smacking his lips.

'Listen to me,' said Mr Henchy. 'What we want in this country, as I said to old Ward, is capital. The King's coming here will mean an influx of money into this country. The citizens of Dublin will benefit by it. Look at all the factories down by the quays there, idle! Look at all the money there is in the country if we only worked the old industries, the mills, the shipbuilding yards and factories. It's capital we want.'

'But look here, John,' said Mr O'Connor. 'Why should we welcome the king of England? Didn't Parnell himself ...'

'Parnell,' said Mr Henchy, 'is dead. Now, here's the way I look at it. Here's this chap come to the throne after his old mother keeping him out of it till the man was grey. He's a man of the world, and he means well by us. He's a jolly fine decent fellow, if you ask me, and no damn nonsense about him. He just says to himself: "The old one never went to see these wild Irish. By Christ, I'll go myself and see what they're like." And are we going to insult the man when he comes over here on a friendly visit? Eh? Isn't that right, Crofton?'

Mr Crofton nodded his head.

'But after all now,' said Mr Lyons argumentatively, 'King Edward's life, you know, is not the very ...'

'Let bygones be bygones,' said Mr Henchy. 'I admire the man personally. He's just an ordinary knockabout like you and me. He's fond of his glass of grog and he's a bit of a rake, perhaps, and he's a good sportsman. Damn it, can't we Irish play fair?'

'That's all very fine,' said Mr Lyons. 'But look at the case of Parnell now.'

'In the name of God,' said Mr Henchy, 'where's the analogy between the two cases?'

'What I mean,' said Mr Lyons, 'is we have our ideals. Why, now, would we welcome a man like that? Do you think now after what he did Parnell was a fit man to lead us? And why, then, would we do it for Edward the Seventh?'

'This is Parnell's anniversary,' said Mr O'Connor, 'and don't let us stir up any bad blood. We all respect him now that he's dead and gone – even the Conservatives,' he added, turning to Mr Crofton.

Pok! The tardy cork flew out of Mr Crofton's bottle. Mr Crofton got up from his box and went to the fire. As he returned with his capture, he said in a deep voice:

'Our side of the house respects him, because he was a gentleman.'

'Right you are, Crofton!' said Mr Henchy fiercely. 'He was the only man that could keep that bag of cats in order. "Down, ye dogs! Lie down, ye curs!" That's the way he treated them. Come in, Joe! Come in!' he called out, catching sight of Mr Hynes in the doorway.

Mr Hynes came in slowly.

'Open another bottle of stout, Jack,' said Mr Henchy. 'Oh, I forgot there's no corkscrew! Here, show me one here and I'll put it at the fire.'

The old man handed him another bottle and he placed it on the hob.

'Sit down, Joe,' said Mr O'Connor; 'we're just talking about the Chief.'

'Ay, ay!' said Mr Henchy.

Mr Hynes sat on the side of the table near Mr Lyons but said nothing.

'There's one of them anyhow,' said Mr Henchy, 'that didn't renege him. By God, I'll say that for you, Joe! No, by God, you stuck to him like a man!'

'Oh, Joe,' said Mr O'Connor suddenly. 'Give us that thing you wrote – do you remember? Have you got it on you?'

'Oh, ay!' said Mr Henchy. 'Give us that. Did you ever hear that, Crofton? Listen to this now: splendid thing.'

'Go on,' said Mr O'Connor. 'Fire away, Joe.'

Mr Hynes did not seem to remember at once the piece to which they were alluding, but, after reflecting a while, he said:

'Oh, that thing, is it …? Sure, that's old now.'

'Out with it, man!' said Mr O'Connor

''Sh, 'sh,' said Mr Henchy. 'Now, Joe!'

Mr Hynes hesitated a little longer. Then amid the silence he took off his hat, laid it on the table and stood up. He seemed to be rehearsing the piece in his mind. After a rather long pause he announced:

THE DEATH OF PARNELL
6 October 1891

He cleared his throat once or twice and then began to recite:

He is dead. Our Uncrowned King is dead.
O, Erin, mourn with grief and woe
For he lies dead whom the fell gang
Of modern hypocrites laid low.

He lies slain by the coward hounds
He raised to glory from the mire;
And Erin's hopes and Erin's dreams
Perish upon her monarch's pyre.

In palace, cabin or in cot
The Irish heart where'er it be
Is bowed with woe – or he is gone
Who would have wrought her destiny.

He would have had his Erin famed,
The green flag gloriously unfurled,
Her statesmen, bards and warriors raised
Before the nations of the World.

He dreamed (alas 'twas but a dream!)
Of Liberty: but as he strove
To clutch that idol, treachery
Sundered him from the thing he loved.

Shame on the coward, caitiff hands
That smote their Lord or with a kiss
Betrayed him to the rabble-rout
Of fawning priests – no friends of his.

May everlasting shame consume
The memory of those who tried
To befoul and smear the exalted name
Of one who spurned them in his pride.

He fell as fall the mighty ones,
Nobly undaunted to the last,
And death has now united him
With Erin's heroes of the past.

No sound of strife disturbs his sleep!
Calmly he rests: no human pain
Or high ambition spurs him now
The peaks of glory to attain.

> *They had their way: they laid him low.*
> *But Erin, list, his spirit may*
> *Rise, like the Phoenix from the flames,*
> *When breaks the dawning of the day,*
>
> *The day that brings us Freedom's reign*
> *And on that day may Erin well*
> *Pledge in the cup she lifts to Joy*
> *One grief – the memory of Parnell.*

Mr Hynes sat down again on the table. When he had finished his recitation, there was a silence and then a burst of clapping: even Mr Lyons clapped. The applause continued for a little time. When it had ceased, all the auditors drank from their bottles in silence.

Pok! The cork flew out of Mr Hynes' bottle, but Mr Hynes remained sitting flushed and bare-headed on the table. He did not seem to have heard the invitation.

'Good man, Joe!' said Mr O'Connor, taking out his cigarette-papers and pouch the better to hide his emotion.

'What do you think of that, Crofton?' cried Mr Henchy. 'Isn't that fine? What?'

Mr Crofton said that it was a very fine piece of writing.

LITTLE TIM BRANNEHAN

by Lord Dunsany

EITHER TO DECEIVE THE Germans in case they should come, or some more local enemy, the people of Sheehanstown had twisted sideways the arms of the signpost that is a mile from their village; and as some years later, when I came that way in a car, the arms had not yet been put straight, I asked the way of an old man who chanced to be walking by. And one thing leading to another we got into conversation, and I asked him how things were in those parts. 'Terrible, terrible,' said the old man. 'Sure, they're terrible. And it's the same in the whole world, too. It's all going to ruin.'

'As bad as that?' I said.

'Aye,' he answered. 'And worse.'

'And what do you think is the cause of it?' I asked.

'It's all those inventions that they make,' he replied. 'Sure, I can remember when bicycles were new. But that wasn't enough for them, and they must go on till they invented aeroplanes and wireless and I don't know what all. And no good came of it, and the hearts of men has corrupted. Listen now, and I'll tell you. Did you ever hear of the house and family of Blackcastle? No, well, I was thinking you came from a very

long way away. And once there was no country in the world
that hadn't heard of them; but they're all ruined now. And it
happened like this: the estates fell into the hands of a young
Lord Blackcastle, that had a hard, dry, withered heart. So that
was the end of their greatness, for no man can be great with a
hard heart. Aye, that was the end of them. God be with the old
days.'

'What did he do?' I asked.

'Do, is it?' he said. 'Sure, he had a hard, withered heart.
What could he do?'

'Did he commit a crime?' I asked.

'Begob, it was worse nor a crime,' he said. 'Sure, you
wouldn't mind a bit of crime in a man. He grudged a sup of
milk to a child.'

'He shouldn't have done that,' I said.

'It's what he did,' said the old man.

'How did it happen?' I asked.

'Sure, the good Lady Blackcastle, that had been his
mother, died,' he said, 'and there was nobody to look after
him then. And he went abroad, and he went from bad to
worse, and he comes home, and that's what he did. Mustn't a
man have a black heart in him indeed to grudge a glass of
milk to an ailing child?'

'Are you sure he did it?' I asked. 'And did he mean to?'

'Did it!' he said. 'And mean to! Sure the whole thing's
down in writing. Look now. It's in my pocket. I have it there
night and day. Can you read that?'

And he pulled out an envelope holding a half sheet of
notepaper, with writing in faded ink; and crumpled and
thumbed though it was, I could still read the old writing. 'Let
a pint of milk a day,' it said, 'be given to little Tim Brannehan,
since he is weakly. Moira Blackcastle.'

He gave me time to read it and time for the import of the
note to sink in, as he stood before me, a tall, white-bearded,
reproachful figure, looking at the evidence which I held in my
hand of the ruin that was coming to the world.

'He comes home from abroad,' he said, 'and goes into his
dairy, and he stops that pint of milk being given out any more.
And I shows him that very letter. And it has no more effect on

him than a snowflake in the face of a charging bull or a wild lion. And you have seen the letter yourself, and a man must have a hard, black heart to go against a letter like that, written by such a lady as was Lady Blackcastle, now in heaven among the blessed saints. Sure, the world's going to ruin.'

'But when did all this happen?' I asked. 'And who is little Tim Brannehan?'

'Sure, it happened only the other day,' he said. And the old man drew himself up to his full height, straightening for a moment the limbs that the years had bent. 'And do you think I don't know what I'm talking about? Sure, I'm Tim Brannehan. And I was never refused that milk for seventy years.'

HOMEWARD

by Cyril Daly

TO GIVE HIM HIS due, the canon felt guilty when he told the lie. Telling a lie to an ordinary man was one thing, but telling it to a Jesuit was a different kettle of fish altogether. And he surprised himself how easy he was able to tell it. No bother at all. You'd think he'd been at if for years.

'That's all then, Canon, on the west side of Durras?' the Jesuit said, drawing a fastidious napkin across his lips.

'That's all, and you've plenty work in them five, I can tell you. They're all hard nuts.'

'No one else you'd like me to see? Quite sure now?' You'd think the Jesuit knew about Connie Clinch. And he looked so eager to go, uneasy as a horse rearing for the road. He had green eyes that looked straight into your face and out the back of your skull.

'I'm quite sure. There's no one else I'm worried about,' the canon said. No cock crew, but the clock on the mantelpiece chimed, punctuating the lie. Canon Maloney tried to conduct a private disputation. Maybe it wasn't really a lie. Just a gentle deception. It'd take the Jesuit to get him out of that problem, and the Jesuit was the last man on earth he wanted to know about it.

Canon Maloney had decided he'd never again tell any mission priest about Connie Clinch. He knew what would happen, because it was the same every year. Tell any one of them – Franciscan, Dominican, Passionist, Augustinian, Carmelite or Jesuit – that you had a fellow in the parish who hadn't darkened the church door for forty years, and it was like putting a match to dynamite. They'd galvanise into action, and, armed with prayer and fasting, they'd attack the citadel of Beelzebub in the form of Connie Clinch.

The results were always the same – bleak failure. Connie would be nice to them and he'd even ask them in for a cup of tea, but they never brought him an inch nearer the church.

So the canon was determined. God between any missionary and Connie Clinch. The order for the like of Connie hadn't been founded yet. And the canon wasn't parish priest of Durras for twenty-five years without knowing his own stretch of river. Connie was a cute old trout, who wouldn't be played neatly in by any passing spiritual angler. Too many had tried and failed.

The canon had his own approach to Connie. When they met, as they often did, they'd have a chat about the match last Sunday or the way the potatoes were springing up or the new tractor that John Sullivan got. The canon never mentioned hell or heaven or death or confession. He was a shrewd old angler and a great believer in God's good time.

The first morning of the mission, Connie was in his garden watching the road from Durras. He knew the missionary would come to him first. He was letting on to be busy with his rose bushes, but in reality he was looking forward to the impending battle for his soul.

He hadn't long to wait. The Jesuit came pushing up the hill on the curate's new bike. Connie was silently marshalling his arguments which dispensed with God and explained the universe.

'Good morning,' the Jesuit said. 'Could you put me right for Gortnagapall?'

'Up to the yellow garage a half-mile farther on, then take the second on your right by Jer Hickey's field.'

'Fine roses you have there.'

'They're not bad, I suppose.

'Any trouble with greenfly?'

'I throw tea leaves on them, and divil the greenfly I see on them.'

'The nicotine, I suppose. There's nicotine in tea leaves, isn't there?' the Jesuit said.

'I'm not sure what it is, but it does the trick anyway. You know a fair bit about roses yourself.'

'A little. I had TB five years ago, and when I was convalescing, they gave me the rose garden to look after. I got to like them. We must have a chat about them sometime.'

'I always enjoy a bit of a yarn about them, but there's very few in these parts knows anything about them.'

'I tell you what – when you're coming to the mission tonight, bring down a few of different varieties and see if I can identify them. Mind you, no bets, but I'll have a fair try. I'll see you then.'

And so the Jesuit was gone, leaving Connie in a state of utmost anguish. He had been prepared for sin, death like a thief in the night, the last day, and Satan. He was geared up for the fact that life is short, eternity long, and here we have no resting place. In fact, he was ready to deal with all the cosmic realities. But he hadn't been quite ready for roses and greenfly.

What really worried him was the fact that he had given his word about going down to the church tonight. What would everybody say? Connie was an institution in Durras, a sort of local celebrity. After all, it isn't every parish in Ireland has a man that'll fly in the face of God for forty years.

To be perfectly truthful, Connie's pride was a bit bruised too. The priest had spoken to him as if he was as innocent as an altar boy. Surely the Jesuit must have known. What was he doing, then, talking about roses and nicotine and then pedalling off to see minor delinquents who hadn't been to the sacraments for a year or two?

He decided on a plan of action. He'd go down to the church as he promised, but he'd go by the back way into the sacristy, he'd have a few words with the priest, then he'd clear off as fast as he could.

At a quarter to eight exactly – nice and early so that none

of the men would see him – Connie Clinch free-wheeled down
from his house into the village of Durras. As soon as he passed
the barracks, he put both feet on the ground because his
brakes needed a little attention. The sparks flew from the
studs on his boots, and just as he reached the church, he
swung round to a stop. He threw his bike against the yellow,
dashed wall and crunched his way across the pebbles to the
sacristy.

Holy Jamesie, the sacristan, was there with red sore eyes
and no lips at all.

'Great God, Connie Clinch, what has you in here?'

'Mindin' me own business, Jamesie boy, and maybe you'd
do the same. Is your man here?'

'The canon won't be here ...'

'Don't mind your canon. It's the other fella I'm after.'

Just then the other fella appeared at the door with the
black, vestigial wings hanging from his shoulders.

'Terribly good of you to come down so early. We can have
a chat in here,' he said, showing Connie into the tiny committee room. As Connie walked past Jamesie, he whispered between his yellow teeth, 'One word of this to anybody, Jamesie
boy, an' I'll smash your brains out, so I will.'

'Certainly that's Ena Harkness. No mistake about that.
Right.'

'You're right. Now that one.'

'Super Star.'

'Super Star it is. Try that.'

'Perfecta. Am I right?'

'Right again. You're no fool on the road. Now the last
one.'

'Ah, I'd know it straight away. Vienna Charm.'

'Begad, you know about roses all right and no mistake.'

'That Vienna Charm is a delightful rose.'

'I've only one bush of it, but it's a grand rose all right.'

'We've a whole bed of them up at Rathfarnham,' the Jesuit
said. 'I must get Brother Corrigan to send you half a dozen
bushes in November.'

'Ah, now, I wouldn't like to take advantage.'

'He'd be delighted. What's your address?'

'Connie Clinch, Durras. That'll find me. I'm well known around here.'

'Wonderful to see men like you coming to the mission – the well-known men, I mean. You see, you are observed by the other less enthusiastic parishioners, and they come along too. Don't you agree?'

'Oh, that's a fact. That's a fact.'

'What's this Shakespeare says? "So shines a good deed in a naughty world." You see how percipient the poet was?'

'He was all that.'

'But why on earth do you men stay at the back of the church? Is it shyness or what?'

'It must be shyness keeps us at the back.' Connie felt the back of his head breaking out in tiny hot pin-pricks.

'On the other hand, why should we be shy in the presence of Jesus? He loved to be with sinners, and when all's said and done, aren't we all sinners?'

Connie looked at the Jesuit, at the green, brown-flecked eyes.

'If just a few men came up front, maybe the others would follow suit,' the priest said.

There was a knock on the door. It was Holy Jamesie. 'It's time now, Father.' Connie got up like a flash, eager to make his escape.

'Do you mind if I make a suggestion?' The Jesuit's voice was soft, but there was something in it that struck Connie dumb. 'Why don't you slip out through the sacristy door here and go through the altar rails and then take your place in the front bench. That'll shake them.'

'Oh, holy God, that'd shake them all right,' the sacristan said. Connie looked out at the terrazzo floor of the altar and the tall gold candlesticks and the statue of the Virgin with Holy Jamesie already bustling out to place the roses in glass vases in front of it.

There was nothing for it but to go forward.

The farmers of Durras were there and the shopkeepers and the publicans and the couple of guards and the one remaining saddler. All there. And when they saw Connie Clinch appearing on the altar in front of them, the effect was devastating. Each man doubted his own eyes and his own sanity.

Connie knelt down in the front pew, beads of perspiration running along his palms. He drew both hands down along his thighs to dry them, and he was glad when the priest came out so as the eyes of the congregation would go off him, maybe, for a while.

The church had that initial strangeness of familiar but forgotten things. As the decades of the rosary followed on each other, he was surprised to find his lips moving in involuntary response. The words had a freshness they never had before. The fruit of the womb. The hour of our death. Solid, fundamental, tough. They appealed to him. Then the litany. Tower of Ivory. Ark of the Covenant. Singular Vessel of Devotion. Refuge of Sinners. And the murmured 'Pray for us', 'Pray for us', 'Pray for us'. The words brought back a half-remembered world of mother, wife, and boys. Long ago, long, long ago. Years before the loneliness closed in.

All the same, it was funny to think that he was brought into this church nearly seventy years ago, to the huge font, where the bell-rope hangs. And he made his First Communion there at those wooden rails in front of him. He couldn't remember it clearly, but there was still a vague impression of the Railway Hotel that evening, lemonade and cake, and his father in his Sunday suit. But the Jesuit was talking.

'We'll never become saints in the big things. It's the small things that change the world. Here, my good men, you see a statue of the Virgin; in front of it you see those lovely roses brought here in love by one of yourselves. Now you may say that statue is nothing but so much plaster. And, of course, you would be right. And the flowers are simply part of the economy of nature. Right again.

'But they have been brought together with vision. Vision is the thing. They are a way of honouring the Virgin Mother of Christ, she whom we have just addressed as the Mystical Rose. There is a poem called "Rosa Mystica" which is addressed directly to her. The man who wrote it was not only a poet but a priest also, and a priest, I am glad to say, belonging to my own order:

Tell me the name now, tell me its name:
The heart guesses easily, is it the same?
Mary? The Virgin? Well the heart knows,
She is the mystery, she is that rose.
In the gardens of God, in the daylight divine,
I shall come home to thee, Mother of mine.

'Home, my good men, is where the heart is, where we all long for. And it is worth remembering that in order to come home, we must first wander off. Haven't we all wandered, some of us farther than others? It is good to know that she is waiting for the day we turn back.

'So no matter how far we wander, no matter how black the night of our soul, we can come home to her, Mother of mine. Those words, "Mother of mine", were among the very last uttered by the great and dying Pope John. And why? Because just as the priest had the vision of the poet, so Pope John had the vision of the saint, and they knew what they would find when they found her:

In the gardens of God, in the daylight divine,
I shall worship the wounds with thee, Mother of mine.

'Make no mistake, my men, having found her, we find also the fierce reality of the wounds, the reality of the cross and of the Crucified Christ.'

Afterward, in Paddy Collins' public house the sermon was well discussed.

'A quare sort of sermon that.'

'You'd never hear the oul' canon talkin' like that.'

'Course, the Jesuits are desperate brainy men.'

'Will yeh ever forget th' apparition on the altar?'

'When was he last seen in a church?'

'God only knows. I used hear my father saying it was in the trouble times it begun. A priest said from the altar that any man who took a gun in his hand against the proper government was playing "into the hands of the devil". An', of course, Connie was a mad lunatic of a rebel.'

'He was at the ambush at Crossbarry, wasn't he?'

'And a fearless man they say. Never went near a church since. But a great gunman in his day.'

Connie wasn't there to give his side of the story. He had slipped home, embarrassed beyond measure, as soon as benediction was over. He looked from the porch of his cottage across the valley. A veil of mist was moving along the line of the river. This silence was a terrible thing on a summer evening.

The house was even lonelier than the valley. Kate gone from it for five years now. Five years resting out by the sea, with all belonging to her around her. And the lads. The noise of them. All gone. The world wasn't big enough for the Clinch boys. London, Boston, Providence, Perth. All the noise gone and the clatter and the dirty shoes. All reduced to a card at Christmas.

Two women – mother and wife – had pleaded with him. But his heart was set, the memory of the clerical condemnation was still bright, and he'd bow to no priest. But the Mother of God. She was different. In the first place, she wasn't a priest. An ordinary woman cooking the tea just as Kate had done and looking across the valley with her own thoughts. Mystical Rose. A strange name that. That Jesuit fellow, too. Definitely not the worst of them. Then there was the canon. No great harm in him. He never heard him talking about religion.

Still and all, he wouldn't be trapped. He left the porch and went into the house, and its silence bored through him. The memories of hall and stairs and kitchen. The bed was the only thing for it. He'd sleep it off, and he'd be back to himself in the morning.

But the evening was still bright, and he couldn't sleep. He tossed and turned because he was very warm. Those prayers. And the benediction, all the lights and candles, and the altar boy swinging the golden thing with the smoke, click, click, click, back and forth, like the years swinging by. And the bright ring of metal with the Host inside and the priest holding it up and the little bells ringing. The smell of the smoke. The hymn at the end and all the men singing 'I think of Thee and what Thou art. Thy majesty, Thy state ...'

Oh, it was impossible. He was beyond the beyond. Try and work it out. No Mass of a Sunday, and there were fifty-two Sundays in the year. That was fifty-two mortal sins every year for a start. Multiply that by forty and you've enough sins to damn the world, let alone Connie Clinch. And that was still only the beginning. It was too late now; it was too late for anything. If the canon only knew about the chat he had with the Jesuit, he'd never live it down.

But at that moment the canon was looking absentmindedly at the late news flashes on television, a white mug of drinking chocolate held cosily between his two hands. The Jesuit had only just gone. A shocking man for talking.

There was a sudden short ring on the doorbell.

The canon shuffled across in his slippers to the hall and caught Betty just in time. 'Hi, girl, tell them I'm gone to bed. It's that carnival crowd again wondering about the dodgems or the hobby horses. It'll keep until morning, or is it a nightclub they think I have here?'

He returned to his armchair, and he sipped his drink, not noticing that the television was closed down for the night, and the blank screen flickered beside him. He heard the front door closing.

'Hi, Betty, come here.'

She came in.

'Well?'

'I sent him on his way, Canon.'

'Good girl. That carnival committee think I've nothing to do but stay talking all night. Who was it?'

'Connie Clinch.'

'Con … An' you sent him off?'

'It's after half eleven, Canon.'

Something within the Canon's soul stirred, something planted a long, long time ago by the bishop's hands, never to be stifled by routine or parish or age.

'Oh, sweet God, give me patience with you, Betty girl, or what kind of an eejit are yeh! Go out as fast as your legs will carry you and bring him back here to me. The good angler is on the river, not when most convenient, but when the hungry trout is on the rise.'

Connie looked awkward in the room.

'Good-night, Connie, an' how will the Durras lads do against Kilcrohane on Sunday, do you think?'

'Is it too late in the night for confession, Canon?'

'It's a bit late all right, Connie, but they'll give us time and a half for after hours.'

'Maybe it'd be better if I came back in the mornin'!'

'Please yourself, Connie boy. But they say there's no time like the present.'

'It's a desperate long time, Canon. Forty years. Could you hear a confession like that, or would it have to go to the bishop?'

'What would the bishop know about it, Connie? Sure, that fella hasn't heard a confession this twenty years. Now let's see … we'll begin at the beginning.'

When Connie got up from the prie-dieu, the canon ventured asking, 'You found the Jesuit a good man?' wondering how the missionary had got to the heart of the matter.

'He is a great man for the roses,' was all Connie said. 'But for God Almighty's sake, Canon, don't tell a word of what I told you tonight, because he thinks I'm a pillar of the church. He thinks I'm a terrible innocent man.'

The following morning, the canon and the Jesuit stood outside the church as the men filed out from Mass. Connie came out shyly, the dry taste of the sanctified Host still strange on his tongue.

'There's a great man for roses,' the Jesuit said.

The canon looked at him, but the green eyes told him nothing. The canon gave up. He'd never understand it. Desperate clever men, these Jesuits.

Two of a Kind

by Seán O'Faolain

MAX CREEDON WAS NOT drunk, but he was melancholy-drunk, and he knew it and he was afraid of it.

At first he had loved being there in the jammed streets, with everybody who passed him carrying parcels wrapped in green gold, tied with big red ribbons and fixed with berried holly sprigs. Whenever he bumped into someone, parcels toppled and they both cried 'Oops!' or 'Sorree!' and laughed at one another. A star of snow sank nestling into a woman's hair. He smelled pine and balsam. He saw twelve golden angels blaring silently from twelve golden trumpets in Rockefeller Plaza. He pointed out to a cop that when the traffic lights down Park Avenue changed from red to green the row of white Christmas trees away down the line changed colour by reflection. The cop was very grateful to him. The haze of light on the tops of the buildings made a halo over Fifth Avenue. It was all just the way he knew it would be, and he slopping down from Halifax in that damned old tanker. Then, suddenly, he swung his right arm in a wild arc of disgust.

'To hell with 'em! To hell with everybody!'

'Oops! Hoho, there! Sorree!'

He refused to laugh back.

'Poor Creedon!' he said to himself. 'All alone in New York, on Christmas-bloody-well-Eve, with nobody to talk to, and nowhere to go only back to the bloody old ship. New York all lit up. Everybody all lit up. Except poor old Creedon.'

He began to cry for poor old Creedon. Crying, he reeled through the passing feet. The next thing he knew he was sitting up at the counter of an Eighth Avenue drugstore, sucking black coffee, with one eye screwed up to look out at the changing traffic lights, chuckling happily over a yarn his mother used to tell him long ago about a place called Ballyroche. He had been there only once, nine years ago, for her funeral. Beaming into his coffee cup, or looking out at the changing traffic lights, he went through his favourite yarn about poor Lily:

'Ah, wisha! Poor Lily! I wonder where is she atall, atall now. Or is she dead or alive. It all happened through an Italian who used to be going from one farm to another selling painted statues. Bandello his name was, a handsome black divil o'hell! I never in all my born days saw a more handsome divil. Well, one wet, wild, windy October morning what did she do but creep out of her bed and we all sound asleep and go off with him! Often and often I heard my father say that the last seen of her was standing under the big tree at Ballyroche Cross, sheltering from the rain, at about eight o'clock in the morning. It was Mikey Clancy the postman saw her. "Yerrah, Lily girl," says he, "what are you doing here at this hour of the morning?" "I'm waiting," says she, "for to go into Fareens on the milk cart." And from that day to this not a sight nor a sound of her no more than if the earth had swallowed her. Except for the one letter from a priest in America to say she was happily married in Brooklyn, New York.'

Maxer chuckled again. The yarn always ended up with the count of the years. The last time he heard it, the count had reached forty-one. By this year it would have been fifty.

Maxer put down his cup. For the first time in his life it came to him that the yarn was a true story about a real woman. For as long as four traffic-light changes he fumbled with this fact. Then, like a man hearing a fog signal come again and again from an approaching ship, and at last hearing it close at hand, and then seeing an actual if dim shape wrapped in a cocoon of haze, the great idea revealed itself.

He lumbered down from his stool and went over to the telephones. His lumpish finger began to trace its way down the grey pages among the Brooklyn Bans. His finger stopped. He read the name aloud, 'Bandello, Mrs Lily'. He found a dime, tinkled it home, and dialled the number slowly. On the third ring he heard an old woman's voice. Knowing that she would be very old and might be deaf, he said very loudly and with the extra-meticulous enunciations of all drunks:

'My name is Matthew Creedon. Only my friends all call me Maxer. I come from Limerick, Ireland. My mother came from the townland of Ballyroche. Are you by any chance my Aunt Lily?'

Her reply was a bark:

'What do you want?'

'Nothing at all! Only I thought, if you are the lady in question, that we might have a bit of an ould goster. I'm a sailor. Docked this morning in the Hudson.'

The voice was still hard and cold.

'Did somebody tell you to call me?'

He began to get cross with her.

'Naw! Just by a fluke I happened to look up your name in the directory. I often heard my mother talking about you. I just felt I'd like to talk to somebody. Being Christmas and all to that. And knowing nobody in New York. But if you don't like the idea, it's okay with me. I don't want to butt in on anybody. Good-bye.'

'Wait! You're sure nobody sent you?'

'Inspiration sent me! Father Christmas sent me!' (She could take that any way she bloody-well liked!) 'Look! It seems to me I'm buttin' in. Let's skip it.'

'No. Why don't you come over and see me?'

Suspiciously he said:

'This minute?'

'Right away!'

At the sudden welcome of her voice all his annoyance vanished.

'Sure, Auntie Lily! I'll be right over. But, listen, I sincerely hope you're not thinking I'm buttin' in. Because if you are – '

'It was very nice of you to call me, Matty, very nice indeed. I'll be glad to see you.'

He hung up, grinning. She was just like his mother – the same old Limerick accent. After fifty years. And the same bossy voice. If she was a day, she'd be seventy. She'd be tall, and thin, and handsome, and the real lawdy-daw, doing the grand lady, and under it all she'd be as soft as mountain moss. She'd be tidying the house now like a divil. And giving jaw to ould Bandello. If he was still alive.

He got lost on the subway, so that when he came up it was dark. He paused to have another black coffee. Then he paused to buy a bottle of Jamaica rum as a present for her. And then he had to walk five blocks before he found the house where she lived. The automobiles parked under the lights were all snow-covered. She lived in a brownstone house with high steps. Six other families also had rooms in it.

The minute he saw her on top of the not brightly lit landing, looking down at him, he saw something he had completely forgotten. She had his mother's height, and slimness, and her wide mouth, but he had forgotten the pale, liquid blue of the eyes, and they stopped him dead on the stairs, his hand tight on the banister. At the sight of them he heard the soft wind sighing over the level Limerick plain and his whole body shivered. For miles and miles not a sound but that soughing wind that makes the meadows and the wheat fields flow like water. All over that plain, where a crossroads is an event, where a little, sleepy lake is an excitement. Where their streams are rivers to them. Where their villages are towns. The resting cows look at you out of owls' eyes over the greasy tips of the buttercups. The meadow grass is up to their bellies. Those two pale eyes looking down at him were bits of the pale albino sky stretched tightly over the Shannon plain.

Slowly he climbed up to meet her, but even when they stood side by side, she was still able to look down at him, searching his face with her pallid eyes. He knew what she was looking for, and he knew she had found it when she threw her bony arms around his neck and broke into a low, soft wailing just like that Shannon wind.

'Auntie! You're the living image of her!'

On the click of a finger she became bossy and cross with him, hauling him by his two hands into her room.

'You've been drinking! And what delayed you? And I suppose not a scrap of solid food in your stomach since morning?'

He smiled humbly.

'I'm sorry, Auntie. 'Twas just on account of being all alone, you know. And everybody else making whoopee.' He hauled out the peace offering of the rum. 'Let's have a drink!'

She was fussing all over him immediately.

'You gotta eat something first. Drinking like that all day, I'm ashamed of you! Sit down, boy. Take off your jacket. I got coffee and cookies and hamburgers and a pie. I always lay in a stock for Christmas. All the neighbours visit me. Everybody knows that Lily Bandello keeps an open house for Christmas; nobody is ever going to say Lily Bandello didn't have a welcome for all her friends and relations at Christmastime – '

She bustled in and out of the kitchenette, talking back to him without stop.

It was a big, dusky room, himself looking at himself out of a tall, mirrored wardrobe piled on top with cardboard boxes. There was a divan in one corner as high as a bed, and he guessed that there was a washbasin behind the old peacock-screen. A single bulb hung in the centre of the ceiling, in a fluted glass bell with pink frilly edges. The pope over the bed was Leo XIII. The snowflakes kept touching the bare window-panes like kittens' paws trying to get in. When she began on the questions, he wished he had not come.

'How's Bid?' she called out from the kitchen.

'Bid? My mother? Oh, well, of course, I mean to say– my mother? Oh, she's grand, Auntie! Never better. For her age, of course, that is. Fine, fine out! Just like yourself. Only for the touch of the old rheumatism now and again.'

'Go on, tell me about all of them. How's Uncle Matty? And how's Cis? When were you down in Ballyroche last? But, sure, it's all changed now, I suppose, with electric light and everything up to date? And I suppose the old pony and trap is gone years ago? It was only last night I was thinking of Mikey

Clancy the postman.' She came in, planking down the plates, an iced Christmas cake, the coffeepot. 'Go on! You're telling me nothing.'

She stood over him, waiting, her pale eyes wide, her mouth stretched. He said:

'My Uncle Matty? Oh, well, of course, now, he's not as young as he was. But I saw him there last year. He was looking fine. Fine out. I'd be inclined to say he'd be a bit stooped. But in great form. For his age, that is.'

'Sit in. Eat up. Don't mind me. He has a big family now, no doubt?'

'A family? Naturally! There's Tom. And there's Kitty, that's my Aunt Kitty, it is Kitty, isn't it, yes, my Auntie Kitty. And – God, I can't remember the half of them.'

She shoved the hamburgers toward him. She made him pour the coffee and tell her if he liked it. She told him he was a bad reporter.

'Tell me all about the old place!'

He stuffed his mouth to give him time to think.

'They have twenty-one cows. Holsteins. The black and white chaps. And a red barn. And a shelter belt of pines. 'Tis lovely there now to see the wind in the trees, and when the night falls, the way the lighthouse starts winking at you, and – '

'What lighthouse?' She glared at him. She drew back from him. 'Are ye daft? What are you dreaming about? Is it a lighthouse in the middle of the County Limerick?'

'There is a lighthouse! I saw it in the harbour!'

But he suddenly remembered that where he had seen it was in a toyshop on Eighth Avenue, with a farm beyond it and a red barn and small cows, and a train going round and round it all.

'Harbour, Matty? Are ye out of your senses?'

'I saw it with my own two eyes.'

Her eyes were like marbles. Suddenly she leaned over like a willow – just the way his mother used to lean over – and laughed and laughed.

'I know what you're talking about now. The lighthouse on the Shannon! Lord save us, how many times did I see it at night from the hill of Ballingarry! But there's no harbour, Matty.'

'There's the harbour at Foynes!'

'Oh, for God's sake!' she cried. 'That's miles and miles and miles away. 'Tis and twenty miles away! And where could you see any train, day or night, from anywhere at all near Ballyroche?'

They argued it hither and over until she suddenly found that the coffee was gone cold and rushed away with the pot to the kitchen. Even there she kept up the argument, calling out that certainly, you could see Moneygay Castle, and the turn of the River Deel on a fine day, but no train, and then she went on about the stepping-stones over the river, and came back bubbling about Normoyle's bull that chased them across the dry river, one hot summer's day –

He said:

'Auntie! Why the hell did you never write home?'

'Not even once?' she said, with a crooked smile like a bold child.

'Not a sight nor a sound of you from the day you left Ballyroche, as my mother used to say, no more than if the earth swallowed you. You're a nice one!'

'Eat up!' she commanded him, with a little laugh and a tap on his wrist.

'Did you always live here, Auntie Lily?'

She sat down and put her face between her palms with her elbows on the table and looked at him.

'Here? Well, no – That is to say, no! My husband and me had a house of our very own over in East Fifty-eight. He did very well for himself. He was quite a rich man when he died. A big jeweller. When he was killed in an aeroplane crash five years ago, he left me very well off. But sure I didn't need a house of my own and I had lots of friends in Brooklyn, so I came to live here.'

'Fine! What more do you want, that is for a lone woman! No family?'

'I have my son. But he's married, to a Pole, they'll be over here first thing tomorrow morning to take me off to spend Christmas with them. They have an apartment on Riverside

Drive. He's the manager of a big department store, Macy's on Flatbush Avenue. But tell me about Bid's children. You must have lots of brothers and sisters. Where are you going from here? Back to Ireland? To Limerick? To Ballyroche?'

He laughed.

'Where else would I go? Our next trip we hit the port of London. I'll be back like an arrow to Ballyroche. They'll be delighted to hear I met you. They'll be asking me all sorts of questions about you. Tell me more about your son, Auntie. Has he a family?'

'My son? Well, my son's name is Thomas. His wife's name is Catherine. She's very beautiful. She has means of her own. They're very happy. He's very well off. He's in charge of a big store, Sears, Roebuck on Bedford Avenue. Oh, a fine boy. Fine out! As you say. Fine out. He has three children. There's Cissy, and Matty. And—'

Her voice faltered. When she closed her eyes, he saw how old she was. She rose and from the bottom drawer of a chest of drawers she pulled out a photograph album. She laid it in front of him and sat back opposite him.

'That is my boy.'

When he said he was like her, she said he was very like his father. Maxer said that he often heard that her husband was a most handsome man.

'Have you a picture of him?'

She drew the picture of her son towards her and looked down at it.

'Tell me more about Ballyroche,' she cried.

As he started into a long description of a harvest at home, he saw her eyes close again, and her breath came more heavily and he felt that she was not hearing a word he said. Then, suddenly, her palm slapped down on the picture of the young man, and he knew that she was not heeding him any more than if he wasn't there. Her fingers closed on the pasteboard. She shied it wildly across the room, where it struck the glass of the window flat on, hesitated, and slid to the ground. Maxer saw snowflakes melting as often as they touched the pane. When he looked back at her, she was leaning across the table, one white lock down over one eye, her yellow teeth bared.

'You spy!' She spat at him. 'You came from them! To spy on me!'

'I came from friendliness.'

'Or was it for a ha'porth of look-about? Well, you can go back to Ballyroche and tell 'em whatever you like. Tell 'em I'm starving if that'll please 'em, the mean, miserable, lousy set that never gave a damn about me from the day I left 'em. For forty years my own sister, your mother, never wrote one line to say – '

'You know damn well she'd have done anything for you if she only knew where you were. Her heart was stuck in you. The two of you were inside one another's pockets. My God, she was forever talking and talking about you. Morning, noon, and night – '

She shouted at him across the table.

'I wrote six letters – '

'She never got them.'

'I registered two of them.'

'Nobody ever got a line from you, or about you, only for the one letter from the priest that married you to say you were well and happy.'

'What he wrote was that I was down and out. I saw the letter. I let him send it. That Wop left me flat in this city with my baby. I wrote to everybody – my mother, my father, to Bid after she was your mother and had a home of her own. I had to work every day of my life. I worked today. I'll work to-morrow. If you want to know what I do, I clean out offices. I worked to bring up my son, and what did he do? Walked out on me with that Polack of his and that was the last I saw of him, or her, or any human being belonging to me until I saw you. Tell them every word of it. They'll love it!'

Maxer got up and went over slowly to the bed for his jacket. As he buttoned it, he looked at her glaring at him across the table. Then he looked away from her at the snowflakes feeling the windowpane and dying there. He said quietly:

'They're all dead. As for Limerick – I haven't been back to Ireland for eight years. When my mum died, my father got married again. I ran away to sea when I was sixteen.'

He took his cap. When he was at the door, he heard a

chair fall and then she was at his side, holding his arm, whispering gently to him:

'Don't go away, Matty.' Her pallid eyes were flooded. 'For God's sake, don't leave me alone with them on Christmas Eve!'

Maxer stared at her. Her lips were wavering as if a wind were blowing over them. She had the face of a frightened girl. He threw his cap on the bed and went over and sat down beside it. While he sat there like a big baboon, with his hands between his knees, looking at the snowflakes, she raced into the kitchen to put on the kettle for rum punch. It was a long while before she brought in the two big glasses of punch, with orange sliced in them, and brown sugar like drowned sand at the base of them. When she held them out to him, he looked first at them, and then at her, so timid, so pleading, and he began to laugh and laugh – a laugh that he choked by covering his eyes with his hands.

'Damn ye!' he groaned into his hands. 'I was better off drunk.'

She sat beside him on the bed. He looked up. He took one of the glasses and touched hers with it.

'Here's to poor Lily!' he smiled.

She fondled his free hand.

'Lovie, tell me this one thing and tell me true. Did she really and truly talk about me? Or was that all lies too?'

'She'd be crying rain down when she'd be talking about you. She was always and ever talking about you. She was mad about you.'

She sighed a long sigh.

'For years I couldn't understand it. But when my boy left me for that Polack, I understood it. I guess Bid had a tough time bringing you all up. And there's no one more hard in all the world than a mother when she's thinking of her own. I'm glad she talked about me. It's better than nothing.'

They sat there on the bed talking and talking. She made more punch, and then more, and in the end they finished the bottle between them, talking about everybody either of them had known in or within miles of the County Limerick. They fixed to spend Christmas Day together, and have Christmas dinner downtown, and maybe go to a picture, and then come back and talk some more.

Every time Maxer comes to New York, he rings her number. He can hardly breathe until he hears her voice saying, 'Hello, Matty.'

They go on the town then and have dinner, always at some place with an Irish name; or a green neon shamrock above the door, and then they go to a movie or a show, and then come back to her room to have a drink and a talk about his last voyage, or the picture postcards he sent her, his latest bits and scraps of the news about the Shannon shore. They always get first-class service in restaurants, although Maxer never noticed it until the night a waiter said, 'And what's Mom having?' at which she gave him a slow wink out of her pale Limerick eyes and a slow, wide, lover's smile.

PEASANTS

by Frank O'Connor

WHEN MICHAEL JOHN CRONIN stole the funds of the Carrickna-breena Hurling, Football and Temperance Association, commonly called the Club, everyone said: 'Devil's cure to him!' ''Tis the price of him!' 'Kind father for him!' 'What did I tell you?' and the rest of the things people say when an acquaintance has got what is coming to him.

And not only Michael John but the whole Cronin family, seed, breed and generation, came in for it; there wasn't one of them for twenty miles round or a hundred years back but his deeds and sayings were remembered and examined by the light of this fresh scandal. Michael John's father (the heavens be his bed!) was a drunkard who beat his wife, and his father before him a land-grabber. Then there was an uncle or grand-uncle who had been a policeman and taken a hand in the bloody work at Mitchelstown long ago, and an unmarried sister of the same whose good name it would by all accounts have needed a regiment of husbands to restore. It was a grand shaking-up the Cronins got altogether, and anyone who had a grudge in for them, even if it was no more than a thirty-third cousin, had rare sport, dropping a friendly word about it and saying how sorry he was for the poor mother till he had the blood lighting in the Cronin eyes.

There was only one thing for them to do with Michael John; that was to send him to America and let the thing blow over, and that, no doubt, is what they would have done but for a certain unpleasant and extraordinary incident.

Fr Crowley, the parish priest, was chairman of the committee. He was a remarkable man even in appearance: tall, powerfully built, but very stooped, with shrewd, loveless eyes that rarely softened to anyone except two or three old people. He was a strange man, well on in years, noted for his strong political views, which never happened to coincide with those of any party, and as obstinate as the devil himself. Now what should Fr Crowley do but try to force the committee to prosecute Michael John?

The committee were all religious men who up to this had never as much as dared to question the judgments of a man of God; yes, faith, and if the priest had been a bully, which to give him his due he wasn't, he might have danced a jig on their backs and they wouldn't have complained. But a man has principles, and the like of this had never been heard of in the parish before. What? Put the police on a boy and he in trouble?

One by one the committee spoke up and said so. 'But he did wrong,' said Fr Crowley, thumping the table. 'He did wrong and he should be punished.'

'Maybe so, Father,' said Con Norton, the vice-chairman, who acted as spokesman. 'Maybe you're right, but you wouldn't say his poor mother should be punished too and she a widow-woman?'

'True for you!' chorused the others.

'Serve his mother right!' said the priest shortly. 'There's none of you but knows better than I do the way that young man was brought up. He's a rogue and his mother is a fool. Why didn't she beat Christian principles into him when she had him on her knee?'

'That might be, too,' Norton agreed mildly. 'I wouldn't say but you're right, but is that any reason his Uncle Peter should be punished?'

'Or his Uncle Dan?' asked another.

'Or his cousins, the Dwyers, that keep the little shop in Lissnacarriga, as decent a living family as there is in County Cork?' asked a fourth.

'No, Father,' said Norton, 'the argument is against you.'

'Is it indeed?' exclaimed the priest, growing cross. 'Is it so? What the devil has it to do with his Uncle Dan or his Uncle James? What are ye talking about? What punishment is it to them, will ye tell me that? Ye'll be telling me next 'tis a punishment to me and I a child of Adam like himself.'

'Wisha now, Father,' asked Norton incredulously, 'do you mean 'tis no punishment to them having one of their own blood made a public show? Is it mad you think we are? Maybe 'tis a thing you'd like done to yourself?'

'There was none of my family ever a thief,' replied Fr Crowley shortly.

'Begor, we don't know whether there was or not,' snapped a little man called Daly, a hot-tempered character from the hills.

'Easy, now! Easy, Phil!' said Norton warningly.

'What do you mean by that?' asked Fr Crowley, rising and grabbing his hat and stick.

'What I mean,' said Daly, blazing up, 'is that I won't sit here and listen to insinuations about my native place from any foreigner. There are as many rogues and thieves and vagabonds and liars in Cullough as ever there were in Carricknabreena – ay, begod, and more, and bigger! That's what I mean.'

'No, no, no, no,' Norton said soothingly. 'That's not what he means at all, Father. We don't want any bad blood between Cullough and Carricknabreena. What he means is that the Crowleys may be a fine substantial family in their own country, but that's fifteen long miles away, and this isn't their country, and the Cronins are neighbours of ours since the dawn of history and time, and 'twould be a very queer thing if at this hour we handed one of them over to the police ... And now, listen to me, Father,' he went on, forgetting his rôle of pacifier and hitting the table as hard as the rest, 'if a cow of mine got sick in the morning, 'tisn't a Cremin or a Crowley I'd be asking for help, and damn the bit of use 'twould be to me if

I did. And everyone knows I'm no enemy of the Church but a respectable farmer that pays his dues and goes to his duties regularly.'

'True for you! True for you!' agreed the committee.

'I don't give a snap of my finger what you are,' retorted the priest. 'And now listen to me, Con Norton. I bear young Cronin no grudge, which is more than some of you can say, but I know my duty and I'll do it in spite of the lot of you.'

He stood at the door and looked back. They were gazing blankly at one another, not knowing what to say to such an impossible man. He shook his fist at them.

'Ye all know me,' he said. 'Ye know that all my life I'm fighting the long-tailed families. Now, with the help of God, I'll shorten the tail of one of them.'

Fr Crowley's threat frightened them. They knew he was an obstinate man and had spent his time attacking what he called the 'corruption' of councils and committees, which was all very well as long as it happened outside your own parish. They dared not oppose him openly because he knew too much about all of them and, in public at least, had a lacerating tongue. The solution they favoured was a tactful one. They formed themselves into a Michael John Cronin Fund Committee and canvassed the parishioners for subscriptions to pay off what Michael John had stolen. Regretfully they decided that Fr Crowley would hardly countenance a football match for the purpose.

Then, with the defaulting treasurer, who wore a suitably contrite air, they marched up to the presbytery. Fr Crowley was at his dinner but he told the housekeeper to show them in. He looked up in astonishment as his dining room filled with the seven committee-men, pushing before them the cowed Michael John.

'Who the blazes are ye?' he asked, glaring at them over the lamp.

'We're the Club Committee, Father,' replied Norton.

'Oh, are ye?'

'And this is the treasurer – the ex-treasurer, I should say.'

'I won't pretend I'm glad to see him,' said Fr Crowley grimly.

'He came to say he's sorry, Father,' went on Norton. 'He is sorry, and that's as true as God, and I'll tell you no lie – ' Norton made two steps forward and in a dramatic silence laid a heap of notes and silver on the table.

'What's that?' asked Fr Crowley.

'The money, Father. 'Tis all paid back now and there's nothing more between us. Any little crossness there was, we'll say no more about it, in the name of God.'

The priest looked at the money and then at Norton.

'Con,' he said, 'you'd better keep the soft word for the judge. Maybe he'll think more of it than I do.'

'The judge, Father?'

'Ay, Con, the judge.'

There was a long silence. The committee stood with open mouths, unable to believe it.

'And is that what you're doing to us, Father?' asked Norton in a trembling voice. 'After all the years, and all we done for you, is it you're going to show us up before the whole country as a lot of robbers?'

'Ah, ye idiots, I'm not showing ye up.'

'You are then, Father, and you're showing up every man, woman, and child in the parish,' said Norton. 'And mark my words, 'twon't be forgotten for you.'

The following Sunday Fr Crowley spoke of the matter from the altar. He spoke for a full half hour without a trace of emotion on his grim old face, but his sermon was one long, venomous denunciation of the 'long-tailed families' who, according to him, were the ruination of the country and made a mockery of truth, justice, and charity. He was, as his congregation agreed, a shockingly obstinate old man who never knew when he was in the wrong.

After Mass he was visited in his sacristy by the committee. He gave Norton a terrible look from under his shaggy eyebrows, which made that respectable farmer flinch.

'Father,' Norton said appealingly, 'we only want one word with you. One word and then we'll go. You're a hard character, and you said some bitter things to us this morning; things we never deserved from you. But we're quiet, peaceable poor men and we don't want to cross you.'

Fr Crowley made a sound like a snort.

'We came to make a bargain with you, Father,' said Norton, beginning to smile.

'A bargain?'

'We'll say no more about the whole business if you'll do one little thing – just one little thing – to oblige us.'

'The bargain!' the priest said impatiently. 'What's the bargain?'

'We'll leave the matter drop for good and all if you'll give the boy a character.'

'Yes, Father,' cried the committee in chorus. 'Give him a character! Give him a character!'

'Give him a what?' cried the priest.

'Give him a character, Father, for the love of God,' said Norton emotionally. 'If you speak up for him, the judge will leave off and there'll be no stain on the parish.'

'Is it out of your minds you are, you half-witted angashores?' asked Fr Crowley, his face suffused with blood, his head trembling. 'Here am I all these years preaching to ye about decency and justice and truth and ye no more understand me than that wall there. Is it the way ye want to perjure myself? Is it the way ye want me to tell a damned lie with the name of Almighty God on my lips? Answer me, is it?'

'Ah, what perjure!' Norton replied wearily. 'Sure, can't you say a few words for the boy? No one is asking you to say much. What harm will it do you to tell the judge he's an honest, good-living upright lad, and that he took the money without meaning any harm?'

'My God!' muttered the priest, running his hands distractedly through his grey hair. 'There's no talking to ye, no talking to ye, ye lot of sheep!'

When he was gone the committee-men turned and looked at one another in bewilderment.

'That man is a terrible trial,' said one.

'He's a tyrant,' said Daly vindictively.

'He is, indeed,' sighed Norton, scratching his head. 'But in God's holy name, boys, before we do anything, we'll give him one more chance.'

That evening when he was at his tea, the committee-men

called again. This time they looked very spruce, businesslike, and independent. Fr Crowley glared at them.

'Are ye back?' he asked bitterly. 'I was thinking ye would be. I declare to my goodness, I'm sick of ye and yeer old committee.'

'Oh, we're not the committee, Father,' said Norton stiffly.

'Ye're not?'

'We're not.'

'All I can say is, ye look mighty like it. And, if I'm not being impertinent, who the deuce are ye?'

'We're a deputation, Father.'

'Oh, a deputation! Fancy that, now. And a deputation from what?'

'A deputation from the parish, Father. Now, maybe you'll listen to us.'

'Oh, go on! I'm listening, I'm listening.'

'Well now, 'tis like this, Father,' said Norton, dropping his airs and graces and leaning against the table. ''Tis about that little business this morning. Now, Father, maybe you don't understand us and we don't understand you. There's a lot of misunderstanding in the world today, Father. But we're quiet simple poor men that want to do the best we can for everybody, and a few words or a few pounds wouldn't stand in our way. Now, do you follow me?'

'I declare,' said Fr Crowley, resting his elbows on the table, 'I don't know whether I do or not.'

'Well, 'tis like this, Father. We don't want any blame on the parish or on the Cronins, and you're the one man that can save us. Now all we ask of you is to give the boy a character –'

'Yes, Father,' interrupted the chorus, 'give him a character! Give him a character!'

'Give him a character, Father, and you won't be troubled by him again. Don't say "no" to me now till you hear what I have to say. We won't ask you to go next, nigh or near the court. You have pen and ink beside you and one couple of lines is all you need write. When 'tis over you can hand Michael John his ticket to America and tell him not to show his face in Carricknabreena again. There's the price of his ticket, Father,' he added, clapping a bundle of notes on the table.

'The Cronins themselves made it up and we have his mother's word and his own word that he'll clear out the minute 'tis all over.'

'He can go to pot,' retorted the priest. 'What is it to me where he goes?'

'Now, Father, can't you be patient?' Norton asked reproachfully. 'Can't you let me finish what I'm saying? We know 'tis no advantage to you, and that's the very thing we came to talk about. Now, supposing – just supposing, for the sake of argument – that you do what we say, there's a few of us here, and between us, we'd raise whatever little contribution to the parish fund you'd think would be reasonable to cover the expense and trouble to yourself. Now do you follow me?'

'Con Norton,' said Fr Crowley, rising and holding the edge of the table, 'I follow you. This morning it was perjury, and now 'tis bribery, and the Lord knows what 'twill be next. I see I've been wasting my breath … And I see too,' he added savagely, leaning across the table towards them, 'a pedigree bull would be more use to ye than a priest.'

'What do you mean by that, Father?' asked Norton in a low voice.

'What I say.'

'And that's a saying that will be remembered for you the longest day you live,' hissed Norton, leaning towards him till they were glaring at one another over the table.

'A bull,' gasped Fr Crowley. 'Not a priest.'

''Twill be remembered.'

'Will it? Then remember this too. I'm an old man now. I'm forty years a priest, and I'm not a priest for the money or power or glory of it, like others I know. I gave the best that was in me – maybe 'twasn't much but 'twas more than many a better man would give, and at the end of my days – ' lowering his voice to a whisper, he searched them with his terrible eyes '– at the end of my days, if I did a wrong thing, or a bad thing, or an unjust thing, there isn't man or woman in this parish that would brave me to my face and call me a villain. And isn't that a poor story for an old man that tried to be a good priest?' His voice changed again and he raised his head defiantly.

'Now get out before I kick you out!'

And true to his word and character not one word did he say in Michael John's favour the day of the trial. Three months Michael John got and by all accounts he got off light.

He was a changed man when he came out of jail, downcast and dark in himself. Everyone was sorry for him, and people who had never spoken to him before spoke to him then. To all of them he said modestly: 'I'm very grateful to you, friend, for overlooking my misfortune.' As he wouldn't go to America, the committee made another whip-round and between what they had collected before and what the Cronins had made up to send him to America, he found himself with enough to open a small shop. Then he got a job in the County Council, and an agency for some shipping company, till at last he was able to buy a public house.

As for Fr Crowley, till he was shifted twelve months after, he never did a day's good in the parish. The dues went down and the presents went down, and people with money to spend on Masses took it fifty miles away sooner than leave it to him. They said it broke his heart.

He has left unpleasant memories behind him. Only for him, people say, Michael John would be in America now. Only for him he would never have married a girl with money, or had it to lend to poor people in the hard times, or ever sucked the blood of Christians. For, as an old man said to me of him: 'A robber he is and was, and a grabber like his grandfather before him, and an enemy of the people like his uncle, the policeman; and though some say he'll dip his hand where he dipped it before, for myself I have no hope unless the mercy of God would send us another Moses or Brian Boru to cast him down and hammer him in the dust.'

A PERSIAN TALE

by Lynn Doyle

THE WEE SCHOOLMASTER, BEIN' inclined to a dhrop of whiskey,
an' not gettin' any great encouragement from the ould sister to
take it in his own house, was in the habit of dhroppin' in til
Michael Casshidy's pub most nights; an' to keep the sister
from thinkin' long when he was away, he hit on the notion of
gettin' her a pet of some kind.

Now, though it's mortal hard to explain why, there's a
sthrong fellow feelin' between a cat an' an ould maid; an' afther goin' round as many bastes as would ha' filled a zoo she
fixed her affection on a big cat with a coat on it like a sheep,
that she called a Persian, a conceited useless baste that would
sit washin' an' polishin' at itself with the mice runnin' over it.

But ye never seen womankind yet that wasn't fond of
some useless bein', cat or man; an' for many a long day Paddy
Shaw, as she called him, was the comfort of her heart.

In the end, between the laziness an' him bein' a greedy
gorb of an animal, Paddy grew to a most lamentable size an'
could hardly move about; an' Miss MacDermott got uneasy
about him. The masther said the only thing for him was whiskey, an', troth, himself was well experienced in the same com-
modity.

'Whiskey,' sez the masther, 'is the universal remedy for the male kind. The female sex seems to get on without it in a most remarkable way, but for their lords an' masters there's no medicine to be compared with it.'

Now, I may tell ye, Miss MacDermott had no such notion of the virtues of whiskey as the wee man had – an' small wondher; for it was him had all the fun out of what whiskey was dhrunk in the MacDermott family, an' herself all the bother. But she got terrible fond of the cat, and would ha' done near anythin' to bring it to itself again, so she give in to the masther's notion, an' even went the length of promisin' to pay for any whiskey he bought while the cure was goin' on.

The wee man was terribly pleased about it. He had been what you'd know as off colour for a while before; but he brightened up straight away. At first I thought it was on account of him gettin' his whiskey on the cheap, an', mind ye, that meant somethin'; but all the same it didn't explain why he was takin' so much intherest in the cat. At last he let out the reason himself.

'Ye'll think it strange, Pat,' sez he, 'comin' from a man like myself that has been singin' the praises of whiskey these twenty-five years an' more; but the truth is, a kind of a doubt about the virtues of the immortal liquor has been risin' in my mind this while past.'

'In the name of goodness, Masther,' sez I, 'what has put that notion in your head?'

'It was partly put there by the doctor, that has lattherly been usin' some very alarmin' classical terms in connection with my liver, an' partly by the parish priest, a man,' sez the masther, blinkin' at me a bit droll, 'for whose opinion I have a great deal of respect, not only from his sacred callin', but in his capacity as manager of the Ballygullion National School.

'Now I may tell ye, Pat,' went on the wee man, 'that till lately any misgivin' the pair of them was able to stir up was always scatthered like mornin' mist before the third half-glass of Michael's special.

'But what's worst of all,' sez he, 'for this while past there has been a thraitor in an' about the middle button of my waist-coat basely suggestin' that the effects of our national beverage is not just as beneficent on the system as has been supposed.'

'Ye're never thinkin' of givin' up the whiskey altogether, Masther?' sez I.

'I've been meditatin' it seriously for some time, Pat,' sez he, 'without gettin' much further than that. But I see some chance of comin' to a decision now that I've hit on the great an' scientific notion of thryin' the effects of a dhrop on the cat.'

'How in the name of goodness is that goin' to help ye?' sez I.

'It's as simple as two-times tables,' sez he. 'The only difficulty I had was in the adjustin' of what you might call the alcoholic values between me an' the animal.'

'I don't quite follow ye there,' sez I.

'Wait,' sez he, 'an' I'll explain. I suppose you're aware that the average life of a man is generally taken to be about seventy years?'

'I'm told they lived a deal longer in ould times, Masther,' sez I. 'Did they take a sup then, do ye think?'

'It's undherstood, Pat,' sez the masther, 'that they took a deal of dhrink before the Flood; an' with all that they lived, some of them, to be near a thousand. It's a very consolin' bit of history, for if it proves anythin' at all it's that too much water is just as bad as too much whiskey; an' the case of Noah, though he made his name by water, shows that he didn't think a heap of it as a dhrink. However, seventy years is our average these times, an' seventy years is all a reasonable bein' need aim at.

'Now, as ye know, I'm just fifty-five. If I can stand it another fifteen years, I've had my share, an' barrin' maybe in the matther of whiskey, I've never wanted more than my share. Well, the average life of a cat bein', say, fourteen years, it follows that the vitality of the beast is as five to one compared with a man. Ye got the length of proportion at school, Pat, didn't ye?'

'I did,' sez I, 'afther doin' a lot of damage among canes.'

'Very well,' sez the masther, 'you'll see at once that if the cat can stand three years' whisky, I can stand fifteen, an' that's all I want.'

'How long is he at it now?' sez I. 'An' how is he doin'?'

'He's only six or eight weeks at it yet,' sez the masther, 'an' except in the matther of hair, where the beast is undoubtedly losin' ground, he's doin' beyond my wildest dhreams. Instead of bein' what he used to be, an idle useless drone of a crater, he's skippin' about like a young one, an' killin' mice – aye, an' even rats – like a terrier. I've noticed the same thing with myself, many a time. There I'll be in the school as heavy as dunce, with even vulgar fractions a bother to me: an' before I've been in Michael's half an hour, I can do repeatin' decimals in my head. I admit, mind ye, that the doctor had me a bit daunted a while back; but the outcome of this experiment has been very reassurin'. For anythin' plain an' straightforward like colic or the worms I'll agree with every old woman in the neighbourhood that Dr Dickson has his points; but when he takes it upon him to lay down how far alcohol is beneficial to the human system, the man goes clean beyond his depth.'

An' away trots the wee man up the street with the tall hat cocked over his right eye, an' him whistlin'.

It was a month or more before I met the masther again, an' when I did he was very serious-lookin'.

'Ye find me very low in spirits, Pat,' sez he, noticin' my look. 'The truth is, I'm a bit bothered by the latest results of the investigations at present bein' conducted by myself an' that long-haired divil of a cat. I've been observin' lately that although he's bustlin' about fussy enough afther the mice, when ye look into results, he's missin' a deal more than he's catchin'. An' when I came to apply this observation to my own case, an' put down on paper the sums I told you I could do so well in my head when I was sittin' in Michael's, I found out that though the decimals was repeatin' plenty, the divil a very much of it was the truth. I'm still very far from bein' convinced that whiskey isn't good for the brains, mind ye, Pat; but if the other notion should have come into the head of the P.P. it would be no great advantage to one MacDermott.'

'How could it, Masther,' sez I, 'an' you teachin' like a professor this half a lifetime?'

'There's a little circumstance that has given me some uneasiness on the subject all the same,' sez the masther. 'The sister at home there, though not perhaps in the same scientific way, takes near as much intherest in Paddy as I do myself, but that hasn't kept her from complainin' about the mice a good deal this last while; an' here about a week ago hasn't she installed a lump of a tortoiseshell kitten as what our friends the Presbyterians would call "assistant an' successor". I never thought anythin' of it till comin' down the road the next mornin' doesn't Fr Richard stop me an' suggest that I should appoint big Danny Burke a monitor. He put it to me that he was thinkin' about my health, an' tryin' to make my work a bit easier; but do you know, Pat,' sez the wee man, with the ould comical cock of his eyebrow, 'I wouldn't be surprised if there was as Presbyterian a kind of idea at the back of his head as a parish priest could credibly be supposed to have.

'Come away on down to Michael's,' sez he, 'an' I'll do a bit of experimentin' on myself; for I'm in poor heart this minit.'

About the third wee drop out of Michael's black bottle, he begins to revive.

'Wine, Pat,' sez he, 'maketh glad the heart of man. We have the word of a very wise one on that; an' ye may swear he didn't learn it at second hand. An' I'll go bail if he'd lived in the time of whiskey he'd ha' said the same about that too. If I was only sure it would keep on doin' it, it's a short life an' a merry one I'd go in for, let the docthor say what he likes. But a kind of doubt is creepin' on me even about the fun part of it. It's not lastin' with the cat.'

'Ye told me he was very likely at the first,' sez I.

'At the beginnin', Pat,' sez the masther, 'when I'd got him to the right mixture the noble animal used to go about the house with a smile playin' round his whiskers like the sun on a row of pint bottles. But lattherly his spirits has been goin' down in a way that's not at all encouragin', an' this last week or two ye could hardly live in the house with him.'

'Ye should give him less, Masther,' sez I.

'I can't,' sez he. 'He's carnaptious enough as it is; an' if I dock him of one spoonful of his allowance he gets clean unbearable. He's stopped chasin' his tail, too,' sez the wee man, 'the only bit of light-heartedness he had left. I've been thryin' to persuade myself that it's through him not takin' the same intherest in it now that most of the hair is gone; but still it's a bad sign.

'In my opinion his intellect is failin'. He's beginnin' to have delusions. Every now an' then he'll jump out intil the middle of the kitchen floor as if he was killin' things. I believe it's mice he's seein'. It's only the other night he made a wicked lepp at somethin' he thought he seen, an' near brained himself on the door of the oven.

'The wholly all of it is, Pat, the beast is rangin' himself most damnably on the side of the P.P. I'm beginnin' to see a melancholy prospect of spring water openin' before me. The divil take all cats,' sez he, rappin' on the table for another dhrink; 'for this long-haired curiosity is sthrikin' at the whole foundations of my existence.'

'I'll tell you what I'll do, Masther,' sez I; 'I'll dhrop round the morrow night an' have a look at him. I could find out somethin' else the matter with him than the dhrink.'

'If ye can, Pat,' sez the wee man, shakin' me by the hand, 'I'll put the whole resources of Michael's bar at your disposal, an' carry ye home myself. But I misdoubt when ye clap eyes on the dirty brute ye'll come to the same dismal conclusion about him as myself. Good night now, an' don't forget what ye said.'

I was just danderin' quietly home to shire my head a bit before encountherin' the wife, when who should come up behind me but Dr Dickson. Divil a word of a good night or anythin' else he said, but just into me like a day's work.

'I seen ye comin' out of the public house with the masther, Murphy,' sez he. 'Do ye know that you're assistin' that decent foolish wee body to commit suicide?'

'Bless my soul, Docthor,' sez I, 'ye don't mean to say it's as bad as that with him.'

'I do then,' sez he, very short, 'the man's liver is nearly rotted away with the poison he's been puttin' into him these twenty years, with you an' the like of ye eggin' him on. Ye should be ashamed of yourself, Murphy. I thought betther of ye than that.'

'Ye may think betther than that of me still, Docthor,' sez I. 'I know he's been doin' himself harm this long time. But he's in the notion of quittin' it, an' I'm goin' up the morrow night to help him in the same direction.'

For I may tell ye that was what was in my head when I offered to go up. An' with that I told him all about the cat.

The docthor turned away his head as I was tellin' him; but I could see the shouldhers of him shakin'.

'There's no doubt,' sez he at the last, 'whether it's the whiskey does it for him or not, he's a comical wee crather. An' it would be doin' a kindness to the whole counthryside as well as himself if we could bring him round again.'

'An' can it be done yet, Docthor?' sez I.

'If he would only stop now,' sez he, ' I believe I could save the liver yet, or at any rate bits of it. Let me think a minit. Do you really believe, Pat,' sez he, afther a bit, 'he's in earnest over this business of the cat?'

'I do,' sez I. 'If the liquor kills the cat, I believe he'll make a big stagger at stoppin' it himself.'

'Very well,' sez the docthor, 'would ye take a cat's life to save a man's?'

'If the wee masther is as bad as ye say – an' I don't doubt ye over it – short of a hangin' matther I'm on for anything,' sez I.

'It's well said,' sez the docthor. 'Then come round by my surgery the morrow night an' I'll give ye a bottle of somethin' to dhrop in the cat's dhrink that'll make a quick an' easy end of him. And if the wee man shows no sign of takin' a lesson by it, ye might near as well give him the rest of the bottle himself; for to be plain with ye,' sez the docthor, very serious-lookin', 'if he doesn't soon alther his way of goin', he's likely to make a poor enough end of it.'

When I looked at the cat the next night, the docthor's words came into my mind, an' troth they were true. The divil a more miserable anatomy of a bein' ye ever looked at in your life. From a big, lazy, sonsy-looking animal with a fleece on him like a Shrop ram he was gathered into a wee miserable dwindlin' crather with not as much hair on him as would ha' made a shavin' brush. I don't mind tellin' ye that the look of him gave my own thoughts a twist in the direction of spring water. For it come into my head that bad an' all as it was for the cat himself, it would ha' been a deal worse if he'd had a wife an' family dependin' on him.

'If the whiskey has done that on him, Masther,' sez I, 'he's no great advertisement for it.'

'There's no denyin' that he's gettin' to be a very uncomfortable-lookin' crony to take a dhrink along with,' sez the masther, blinkin' at him very sober. 'If ye can find nothin' else the matther with him, I misdoubt the takin's of Michael Casshidy's bar is goin' down one of these days with a wallop. But wait till ye see the change on him when he gets a sup. Here, Paddy, Paddy,' sez he, an' reaches down a saucer.

Sure enough there was a wondherful change come on the brute the minit he seen it. Up went the ould moth-eaten tail over his back as if he was a kitten again; and though ye'd ha' thought by the look of him a minit before he wouldn't have budged from where he was lyin' if the house was on fire, he was at the saucer in two lepps an' over the whiskers in it before it was well on the floor.

'It's a horrid pity, Pat,' sez the masther, 'that any doubt of the virtues of the stuff should be creepin' on the cowld stomachs of the present generation, for there's no denyin' it's the great medicine. Look at the poor benighted crather that hasn't near the intelligence an' none of the book learnin' of a man like me, an' even himself would hardly lift his head from the saucer if ye tould him the next minit was to be his last.'

There was more truth in the wee man's words than he knowed. As he went into the panthry for two glasses, I emptied the doctor's bottle into the saucer. The cat took about three more laps at it, shook his head, give back a step, an' rolled on the floor.

'Masther,' I shouts, 'Masther! come here quick. The cat's gone.'

An' sure enough before the masther got the length of where he was lyin', poor Paddy was as dead as Hecthor.

The masther straightened himself up afther a long look at him, went over to the dhresser where he had a gallon jar sittin', an' poured himself out a rozener that if the cat had got it would ha' saved Dr Dickson the expense of a bottle. I could hear the tumbler rattlin' again' his teeth as the stuff went down. When he turned round, he was very white an' washy-lookin'.

'I'm sorry about the brute, Pat,' sez he, afther a minit or two. 'Not because he's dead; for the way things was goin' with him, it was in my mind to step down to the docthor's one of these nights an' give him a speedy release; but it's at the back of my head that maybe I didn't give him fair play. Well, it's past prayin' for now, like many another thing, an' we'll let it go. First of all, by way of carryin' out the funeral customs of this island, an' next, to celebrate his memory, we'll just have a thimbleful apiece.'

'I'll put this stuff out of the road first,' thinks I to myself, liftin' the saucer an' throwin' the contents of it in the fire.

When I looked at the wee masther, he was layin' down his glass. There was just what ye'd know of colour come into his face, an' when he spoke it was the ould masther again.

'It's three months, Pat,' sez he, 'since the late lamented an' myself embarked on this experiment, an' five times three is fifteen. That gives me till October is a year. I'll turn it over in my mind for a minit or two, an' in the meantime we'll carry out a great an' appropriate notion that came into my head as I watched ye there pourin' that saucerful of good dhrink on the fire.

'When I had made up my accounts to finish off my deceased unfortunate colleague, I was greatly bothered about the question of his last rites. To give him Christian burial was clean out of the question; for as far as I could see there was no hope of him dyin' in a state of grace. Then takin' into account that the ould Egyptians considhered the cat a sacred animal, I thought of thryin' their way of it; but the divil a thing I knowed about embalmin' – which was the way they done it – no more than my grandmother; an' to pickle the beast would be to make a very scaresome-lookin' corpse of him. But watchin' ye just now, as I said, it come on me like a flash that we'd pay him our last respects in the ancient Roman manner.'

'An' what else would that be but Christian burial, Masther?' sez I.

'It's another kind of Romans that's in my mind, Pat,' sez he, 'an older branch of the family. Away out to the coal-hole an' bring a good armful of sticks an' shavin's to the foot of the garden, an' I'll show ye how it's done.

'Now, Pat,' sez the wee man, layin' the cat on the top of the sticks, 'put a match to the shavin's, till I go back for the rest of the materials.'

By the time I heard him behind me, there was nothin' left of poor Paddy but the bones; an' when I looked round, the masther was comin' down the garden with the gallon jar in one hand an' two tumblers in the other.

'It was the practice of the same Romans, Pat,' sez he, 'when they had burned the corpse of the deceased, to put out the fire with a drop of the very best – or rather, Misther Murphy,' sez he, blinkin' in the firelight, 'with the best the poor benighted heathen knew about, havin' in those days nothin' more satisfactory to dhrink than a cowld splash of wine. An' though I don't find it in the books, there's no manner of doubt that, such as it was, they took a jorum at the same time just to dhrive away sorrow. So we'll do the full rites by poor Paddy.' With that he sets the tumblers on the ground an' pours out two stiff ones.

'Stand back now, Pat,' sez he; an' before I knowed what he was afther, he had cowped the gallon jar on the fire. The flames went up with a woof! would ha' frightened ye, an' for a minit I thought the masther was desthroyed; but when I thrailed him back, barrin' the nap on his tall hat, he wasn't a thraneen the worse.

'Didn't I tell ye?' sez he. 'The divil an ancient Roman ever seen a flame like that in his life. It's the great stuff – gimme my glass – an here's Paddy Shaw's memory in the last dhrop – worse luck – I'll ever taste of it.'

BIRD MILLIGAN

by Oliver St John Gogarty

THIS IS HOW HE got his nickname, the Bird. He went to a fancy-dress ball at a roller-skating rink dressed in a kind of loose garment or robe. He was supported by two holy women. When the dancing was in full swing, he laid an egg as big as a football, flapped his wings and chortled. The manager threw him out and the holy women with him. But he was Bird Milligan from that day. He was called the Bird by so many people that his other name was forgotten.

Dublin is not like Paris, where they say that, in the garden of the Tuileries, knights in armour are to be seen sitting with one-eyed pirates, and nobody takes any notice even of the man with the crossbow who assures everyone that he was the man who killed King Richard the Lion-Heart. Nevertheless Dublin has, if not paranoiacs, eccentrics surely. It was Boyle Tisdall Stewart Fitzgerald Farrell, who was called Endymion because he was touched by the moon. He caricatured in his own person anything of which he disapproved. He carried two sabres and wore starched cuffs on his ankles to show that the world was upside-down. Sometimes he made a nuisance of himself by going into the public library and entering all his names in the book. That done, he left muttering. Then there

was Professor Maginni, Professor of Deportment. His idea of
deportment caused him to dress in a dark brown frock coat,
striped trousers, brown shoes, top hat, and waxed moustache.
He walked mincingly. He walked about for business purposes.
His real name was Maginnis. Evidently he thought that
Maginni gave his name an Italian flourish all the more useful
for business purposes. No one could accuse the Bird of acting
for business purposes. It would be very hard to see anything
faintly resembling business in the laying of an egg.

The Bird retired for a month to his farm near Dublin. People said that he was engaged in breaking in young horses. He
had the reputation of being a good horseman. It is hard to say
how these rumours got about. Perhaps because his nose was
broken by a horse throwing his head back suddenly. To suffer
such an accident he must have spent his time among young
horses, and hostlers' talk in the taverns did the rest. He certainly had a buggy with a fine horse in the shafts when he
appeared in town. By that two-wheeler hangs a tale. He and a
young woman were seen driving up the slope of Portobello
Bridge. They were evidently quarrelling, for the Bird's voice
was raised so that anything the lady said could not be heard.
But the Bird's voice was distinctly heard when the buggy
reached the crest of the bridge, because it halted for a moment
there. 'You have been the pest of my life,' the Bird shouted,
'and it's time it ended.' With that he threw her bodily into the
canal. A policeman in full uniform plunged, helmet and all,
into the water. He swam to the rescue, only to find a dummy
from a shop window in a fashionable part of the town in his
arms. By the time he came out and looked for the Bird, the
Bird had flown.

A complaint was laid, not by the police, but by some
busybody, with the father of the Bird. The Bird's father was an
alderman of the city and a most respectable man. He should
curb his son. Perhaps his father had not looked after the Bird
with due care. It was known that the alderman was a widow-
er, so the busybody argued. His father at last reluctantly consented. He spoke to the Bird, and whatever he said to him, the
Bird went to Canada for a while. But the Bird came back.

If you want to look for the counterpart of the merrie men

of Dublin, you will have to look at some of the characters in Russian novels – Turgenev, for example. But the characters in these novels tend to do dangerous feats which are meaningless. A young man jumps his horse over a precipice where failure means loss of life. They are not truly counterparts.

The Bird was within his rights, and he should not have been thrown out of the skating-rink ball. After all, it was a fancy-dress affair. If the fancy dress represented a bird, it was quite in order to lay an egg. And the manager was in no position to decide how big the egg should be.

During the Bird's absence in Canada, the town depended for its merriment on Endymion; and he did his best. That is doubtless why the Bird's exploits and Endymion's tend to merge, so it is better to know the authors of the different actions that kept the old town amused. Endymion must be credited with the fishing incident. It took place in this way. Dublin has two-decker buses, some of them open at the top. On one of these Endymion stood fishing. He had a salmon rod and a line, at the end of which was a fly as large as a sparrow. Solemnly he cast the fly onto the cement footpath. He waited until some passenger would try to humour him by asking if he had caught anything. Then Endymion would come into his own. 'What, on that?' he would say, pointing to the cement footpath. 'You must be mad!' So that helps us to differentiate between Endymion and the Bird. A further source of confusion comes from the two sabres Endymion carried on occasion to show his disapproval of warfare. The Bird may have borrowed one or provided one himself. After his return from Canada, he went to an Italian warehouse, as the delicatessens were called in Dublin. Hams and flitches of bacon hung suspended from an iron bar high in the air outside the store. One morning before the rush hour the Bird approached the owner of the delicatessen and bought a ham. He got a receipt. After the transaction he asked the proprietor to let the ham hang where it was for a few hours. The Bird had other things to do, and he did not wish to cart the ham around with him. To this the owner consented. At the rush hour the Bird returned. He had a sabre in his hand with which he *addressed* the ham, inviting it to a duel. After a few flourishes he transfixed the ham

and, putting it over his shoulder, ran off. He was closely pur-
sued by two policemen. Cornered at last, the Bird produced
the receipt for the ham and asked was there no liberty left in
the country when a man couldn't buy a ham without being
arrested?

As a result of this exploit, and probably because of a few
others, the Bird was sent to Australia. He pretended that he
went willingly, that it was a country that delighted in horses
and it was just the place for him. But after a few months the
Bird proved to be a homing pigeon. He returned.

Dublin is possessed of a Ballast Office, over the door of
which is a clock which tells sidereal time. Promptly at noon
the Bird took up his station before the clock. When the clock's
hands pointed to the hours, two alarm clocks which the Bird
had in his tail pocket went off together. Much mirth attended
the Bird. He smiled and went off satisfied. He had the exact
time.

All the aldermen of the city, headed by the Lord Mayor,
planned to hold a World's Fair. It would be like nothing on
earth. It was.

Nations from all parts of the globe were invited to show
their wares and to be sure that their national costumes were
represented. The Americas were in it; South Africa and the Far
East, which meant Japan. It was Japan that caused the most
interest. This was largely if not altogether due to a tribe that
were never before beheld by Western eyes. They were the
hairy Ainus, a very primitive tribe who were reputed to go
into dark caves and to fight with bears with nothing but a
knife and a bearskin thrown loosely over their shoulders. The
bear would grapple with the Ainu only to find that the bearskin came off in the fight, during which he was disem-
bowelled. A whole family of hairy Ainus was displayed, children and all. They were copper-coloured, even to the baby in
arms. The baby was not long in arms, for it disappeared mysteriously. Whereupon a truly frightful uproar broke out. Nobody knew what the mother was saying. She was pointing to
her breasts; but nobody understood. The man of the tribe was
desperate. He would have broken loose but for the iron bars
behind which the family was ensconced. At last someone,

probably a member of the Japanese government, said that the baby had disappeared and that, naturally, the parents were frantic. Would no one search for it? If the Ainus broke out ...

At last the baby was found in the French pavilion. It was at long last, for nobody thought of searching there. The baby was found smiling, for it was interested in a bottle of warm milk the like of which it had never seen.

The aldermen held a special meeting. Eyes, unfriendly for the most part, were turned on Alderman Milligan. Was he not directly responsible for getting the corporation of the city in such a jam? Had the baby been found anywhere but in the French pavilion, it might have been a different matter. As it was, the French took the placing of the baby there as a direct insult. Obviously, the reference intended was a reference to their falling birth rate, as well as the fact that the French nation was very high in the scale of infant mortality. An international incident could be made of such an insult. The French consul attended and he took a lot of placating. He forgave the aldermen because it was proved to his satisfaction that none of them was responsible.

The Bird was banished.

Months later, a friend was strolling down a street in Buenos Aires. There was a large hole in the street, at the bottom of which a man was working with a pick. The friend chanced to look down. He thought he recognised the broad shoulders and the red neck, which were out of keeping with the local workmen. 'Good Heavens, Bird, is that you?' The Bird looked up. 'Get to hell out of that! It took a mighty lot of influence to get me this job!'

He was through with bad companions. It may have been due to the difficulty of securing a job or it may not. But there were no more 'incidents' in Dublin.

The first and last I saw of the Bird was in the Phoenix Park, which is said to be the largest park enclosed by a wall in Europe. He must have been pointed out to me, for I never remember meeting him. I saw the nose across his face, the red face and neck, and the well-dressed set-up of the man as he came prancing by on a big bay horse. I saw his light brown waistcoat, his riding gloves, one of which fell over his left wrist, the bowler hat, the riding trousers and boots. He raised his whip in an exaggerated salute and cantered off.

That was long after the changing of the Ainu baby: you cannot call it stealing, for it never left the Fair.

The Bird was of a generous nature; he harmed nobody. Dublin is a lesser place since it lost its men of mirth.

The Miraculous Revenge

by George Bernard Shaw

I ARRIVED IN DUBLIN on the evening of 5 August, and drove to
the residence of my uncle, the cardinal archbishop. He is, like
most of my family, deficient in feeling, and consequently cold
to me personally. He lives in a dingy house, with a side-long
view of the portico of his cathedral from the front windows,
and of a monster national school from the back. My uncle
maintains no retinue. The people believe that he is waited
upon by angels. When I knocked at the door, an old woman,
his only servant, opened it, and informed me that her master
was then officiating in the cathedral, and that he had directed
her to prepare dinner for me in his absence. An unpleasant
smell of salt fish made me ask her what the dinner consisted
of. She assured me that she had cooked all that could be permitted in His Holiness' house on a Friday. On my asking her
further why on a Friday, she replied that Friday was a fast
day. I bade her tell His Holiness that I had hoped to have the
pleasure of calling on him shortly, and drove to a hotel in
Sackville Street, where I engaged apartments and dined.

After dinner I resumed my eternal search – I know not for
what; it drives me to and fro like another Cain. I sought in the
streets without success. I went to the theatre. The music was

execrable, the scenery poor. I had seen the play a month before in London, with the same beautiful artist in the chief part. Two years had passed since, seeing her for the first time, I had hoped that she, perhaps, might be the long-sought mystery. It had proved otherwise. On this night I looked at her and listened to her for the sake of that bygone hope, and applauded her generously when the curtain fell. But I went out lonely still. When I had supped at a restaurant, I returned to my hotel, and tried to read. In vain. The sound of feet in the corridors as the other occupants of the hotel went to bed distracted my attention from my book. Suddenly it occurred to me that I had never quite understood my uncle's character. He, father to a great flock of poor and ignorant Irish; an austere and saintly man, to whom livers of hopeless lives daily appealed for help heavenward; who was reputed never to have sent away a troubled peasant without relieving him of his burden by sharing it; whose knees were worn less by the altar steps than by the tears and embraces of the guilty and wretched; he had refused to humour my light extravagances, or to find time to talk with me of books, flowers, and music. Had I not been made to expect it? Now that I needed sympathy myself, I did him justice. I desired to be with a true-hearted man, and to mingle my tears with his.

I looked at my watch. It was nearly an hour past midnight. In the corridor the lights were out, except one jet at the end. I threw a cloak upon my shoulders, put on a Spanish hat, and left my apartment, listening to the echoes of my measured steps retreating through the deserted passages. A strange sight arrested me on the landing of the grand staircase. Through an open door I saw the moonlight shining through the windows of a saloon in which some entertainment had recently taken place. I looked at my watch again. It was but one o'clock; and yet the guests had departed. I entered the room, my boots ringing loudly on the waxed boards. On a chair lay a child's cloak and a broken toy. The entertainment had been a children's party. I stood for a time looking at the shadow of my cloaked figure upon the floor, and at the disordered decorations, ghostly in the white light. Then I saw that there was a grand piano, still open, in the middle of the room. My fingers throbbed as I sat down before it, and expressed all that I felt in a grand hymn which seemed to thrill the cold stillness of the shadows in a deep hum of approbation, and to people the radiance of the moon with angels. Soon there was a stir without too, as if the rapture was spreading abroad. I took up the chant triumphantly with my voice, and the empty saloon resounded as though to the thunder of an orchestra.

'Hallo, sir!' 'Confound you, sir – ' 'Do you suppose that this – ' 'What the deuce – ?'

I turned, and silence followed. Six men, partially dressed, and with dishevelled hair, stood regarding me angrily. They all carried candles. One of them had a bootjack, which he held like a truncheon. Another, the foremost, had a pistol. The night porter was behind trembling.

'Sir,' said the man with the revolver, coarsely, 'may I ask whether you are mad, that you disturb people at this hour with such an unearthly noise?'

'Is it possible that you dislike it?' I replied, courteously.

'Dislike it!' said he, stamping with rage. 'Why – damn everything – do you suppose we were enjoying it?'

'Take care. He's mad,' whispered the man with the boot-jack.

I began to laugh. Evidently they did think me mad. Unaccustomed to my habits, and ignorant of music as they probably were, the mistake, however absurd, was not unnatural. I rose. They came closer to one another; and the night porter ran away.

'Gentlemen,' I said, 'I am sorry for you. Had you lain still and listened, we should all have been the better and happier. But what you have done, you cannot undo. Kindly inform the night porter that I am gone to visit my uncle, the cardinal archbishop. Adieu!'

I strode past them, and left them whispering among themselves. Some minutes later I knocked at the door of the cardinal's house. Presently a window on the first floor was opened; and the moonbeams fell on a grey head, with a black cap that seemed ashy pale against the unfathomable gloom of the shadow beneath the stone sill.

'Who are you?'

'I am Zeno Legge.'

'What do you want at this hour?'

The question wounded me. 'My dear uncle,' I exclaimed, 'I know you do not intend it, but you make me feel unwelcome. Come down and let me in, I beg.'

'Go to your hotel,' he said sternly. 'I will see you in the morning. Good night.' He disappeared and closed the window.

I felt that if I let this rebuff pass, I should not feel kindly towards my uncle in the morning, nor, indeed, at any future time. I therefore plied the knocker with my right hand, and kept the bell ringing with my left until I heard the door-chain rattle within. The cardinal's expression was grave nearly to moroseness as he confronted me on the threshold.

'Uncle,' I cried, grasping his hand, 'do not reproach me. Your door is never shut against the wretched. I am wretched. Let us sit up all night and talk.'

'You may thank my position and not my charity for your admission, Zeno,' he said. 'For the sake of the neighbours, I had rather you played the fool in my study than upon my doorstep at this hour. Walk upstairs quietly, if you please. My housekeeper is a hardworking woman: the little sleep she allows herself must not be disturbed.'

'You have a noble heart, Uncle. I shall creep like a mouse.'

'This is my study,' he said, as we entered an ill-furnished den on the second floor. 'The only refreshment I can offer you, if you desire any, is a bunch of raisins. The doctors have forbidden you to touch stimulants, I believe.'

'By heaven – !' He raised his finger. 'Pardon me; I was wrong to swear. But I had totally forgotten the doctors. At dinner I had a bottle of *Grave*.'

'Humph! You have no business to be travelling alone. Your mother promised me that Bushy should come over here with you.'

'Pshaw! Bushy is not a man of feeling. Besides, he is a coward. He refused to come with me because I purchased a revolver.'

'He should have taken the revolver from you, and kept to his post.'

'Why will you persist in treating me like a child, Uncle? I am very impressionable, I grant you; but I have gone round the world alone, and do not need to be dry-nursed through a tour in Ireland.'

'What do you intend to do during your stay here?'

I had no plans; and instead of answering I shrugged my shoulders and looked round the apartment. There was a statuette of the Virgin upon my uncle's desk. I looked at its face, as he was wont to look in the midst of his labours. I saw there eternal peace. The air became luminous with an infinite network of the jewelled rings of paradise descending in roseate clouds upon us.

'Uncle,' I said, bursting into the sweetest tears I had ever shed, 'my wanderings are over. I will enter the Church, if you will help me. Let us read together the third part of *Faust*; for I understand it at last.'

'Hush, man,' he said, half rising with an expression of alarm. 'Control yourself.'

'Do not let my tears mislead you. I am calm and strong. Quick, let us have Goethe:

> *Das Unbeschreibliche.*
> *Hier ist getan;*
> *Das Ewig-Weibliche,*
> *Zieht uns hinan.*

'Come, come. Dry your eyes and be quiet. I have no library here.'

'But I have – in my portmanteau at the hotel,' I said, rising. 'Let me go for it, I will return in fifteen minutes.'

'The devil is in you, I believe. Cannot – '

I interrupted him with a shout of laughter. 'Cardinal,' I said noisily, 'you have become profane; and a profane priest is always the best of good fellows. Let us have some wine; and I will sing you a German beer song.'

'Heaven forgive me if I do you wrong,' he said; 'but I believe God has laid the expiation of some sin on your unhappy head. Will you favour me with your attention for a while? I have something to say to you, and I have also to get some sleep before my hour for rising, which is half past five.'

'My usual hour for retiring – when I retire at all. But proceed. My fault is not inattention, but over-susceptibility.'

'Well, then, I want you to go to Wicklow. My reasons – '

'No matter what they may be,' said I, rising again. 'It is enough that you desire me to go. I shall start forthwith.'

'Zeno! Will you sit down and listen to me?'

I sank upon my chair reluctantly. 'Ardour is a crime in your eyes, even when it is shown in your service,' I said. 'May I turn down the light?'

'Why?'

'To bring on my sombre mood, in which I am able to listen with tireless patience.'

'I will turn it down myself. Will that do?'

I thanked him, and composed myself to listen in the shadow. My eyes, I felt, glittered. I was like Poe's raven.

'Now for my reasons for sending you to Wicklow. First, for your own sake. If you stay in town, or in any place where excitement can be obtained by any means, you will be in Swift's Hospital in a week. You must live in the country, under the eye of one upon whom I can depend. And you must have something to do to keep you out of mischief, and away from your music and painting and poetry, which, Sir John Richards writes to me, are dangerous for you in your present morbid state. Second, because I can entrust you with a task which, in the hands of a sensible man, might bring discredit on the Church. In short, I want you to investigate a miracle.'

He looked attentively at me. I sat like a statue.

'You understand me?' he said.

'Nevermore,' I replied hoarsely. 'Pardon me,' I added amused at the trick my imagination had played me, 'I understand you perfectly. Proceed.'

'I hope you do. Well, four miles distant from the town of Wicklow is a village called Four Mile Water. The resident priest is Fr Hickey. You have heard of the miracles at Knock?'

I winked.

'I did not ask you what you think of them, but whether you have heard of them. I see you have. I need not tell you that even a miracle may do more harm than good to the Church in this country, unless it can be proved so thoroughly

that her powerful and jealous enemies are silenced by the
testimony of followers of their heresy. Therefore, when I saw
in a Wexford newspaper last week a description of a strange
manifestation of the Divine Power which was said to have
taken place at Four Mile Water, I was troubled in my mind
about it. So I wrote to Fr Hickey, bidding him give me an
account of the matter if it were true, and if not, to denounce
from the altar the author of the report, and to contradict it in
the paper at once. This is his reply. He says – well, the first
part is about Church matters: I need not trouble you with it.
He goes on to say – '

'One moment. Is that his own handwriting? It does not
look like a man's.'

'He suffers from rheumatism in the fingers of his right
hand, and his niece, who is an orphan, and lives with him, acts
as his amanuensis. Well – '

'Stay. What is her name?'

'Her name? Kate Hickey.'

'How old is she?'

'Tush, man, she is only a little girl. If she were old enough
to concern you, I should not send you into her way. Have you
any more questions to ask about her?'

'None. I can fancy her in a white veil at the rite of con-
firmation, a type of faith and innocence. Enough of her. What
says the Reverend Hickey of the apparitions?'

'They are not apparitions. I will read you what he says.
Ahem!

> In reply to your inquiries concerning the late miraculous
> event in this parish, I have to inform you that I can vouch
> for its truth, and that I can be confirmed not only by the
> inhabitants of the place, who are all Catholics, but by every
> person acquainted with the former situation of the grave-
> yard referred to, including the Protestant archdeacon of
> Baltinglass, who spends six weeks annually in the neigh-
> bourhood, The newspaper account is incomplete and in-
> accurate. The following are the facts: About four years ago,
> a man named Wolfe Tone Fitzgerald settled in this village
> as a farrier. His antecedents did not transpire, and he had
> no family. He lived by himself, was very careless of his per-
> son; and when in his cups, as he often was, regarded the

honour neither of God nor man in his conversation. Indeed
if it were not speaking ill of the dead, one might say that he
was a dirty, drunken, blasphemous blackguard. Worse
again, he was, I fear, an atheist, for he never attended Mass,
and gave his Holiness worse language even than he gave
the Queen. I should have mentioned that he was a bitter
rebel, and boasted that his grandfather had been out in '08,
and his father with Smith O'Brien. At last he went by the
name of Brimstone Billy, and was held up in the village as
the type of all wickedness.

You are aware that our graveyard, situated on the
north side of the water, is famous throughout the country as
the burial place of the nuns of St Ursula, the hermit of Four
Mile Water, and many other holy people. No Protestant has
ever ventured to enforce his legal right of interment there,
though two have died in the parish within my own recollec-
tion. Three weeks ago, this Fitzgerald died in a fit brought
on by drink, and a great hullabaloo was raised in the village
when it became known that he would be buried in the
graveyard. The body had to be watched to prevent its being
stolen and buried at the crossroads. My people were greatly
disappointed when they were told I could do nothing to
stop the burial, particularly as I of course refused to read
any service on the occasion. However, I bade them not
interfere; and the interment was effected on 14 July, late in
the evening, and long after the legal hour. There was no disturbance. Next morning, the graveyard was found moved
to the south side of the water, with the one newly-filled
grave left behind on the north side; and thus they both re-
main. The departed saints would not lie with the reprobate.
I can testify to it on the oath of a Christian priest; and if this
will not satisfy those outside the Church, everyone, as I said
before, who remembers where the graveyard was two
months ago, can confirm me.

I respectfully suggest that a thorough investigation into
the truth of this miracle be proposed to a committee of Protestant gentlemen. They shall not be asked to accept a single
fact of hearsay from my people. The ordnance maps show
where the graveyard was; and anyone can see for himself
where it is. I need not tell your Eminence what a rebuke this
would be to those enemies of the holy Church that have
sought to put a stain on her by discrediting the late wonderful manifestations at Knock Chapel. If they come to Four

Mile Water, they need cross-examine no one. They will be
asked to believe nothing but their own senses.

Awaiting your Eminence's counsel to guide me further
in the matter,
I am, etc.

'Well, Zeno,' said my uncle, 'what do you think of Fr Hickey
now?'

'Uncle, do not ask me. Beneath this roof I desire to believe
everything. The Reverend Hickey has appealed strongly to my
love of legend. Let us admire the poetry of his narrative and
ignore the balance of probability between a Christian priest
telling a lie on his oath and a graveyard swimming across a
river in the middle of the night and forgetting to return.'

'Tom Hickey is not telling a lie, sir. You may take my
word for that. But he may be mistaken.'

'Such a mistake amounts to insanity. It is true that I myself, awaking suddenly in the depth of night, have found myself convinced that the position of my bed has been reversed.
But on opening my eyes the illusion ceased. I fear Fr Hickey is
mad. Your best course is this. Send down to Four Mile Water a
perfectly sane investigator; an acute observer; one whose per-
ceptive faculties, at once healthy and subtle, are absolutely un-
clouded by religious prejudice. In a word, send me. I will report to you the true state of affairs in a few days, and you can
then make arrangements for transferring Hickey from the altar
to the asylum.'

'Yes, I had intended to send you. You are wonderfully
sharp and you would make a capital detective if you could
only keep your mind to one point. But your chief qualification
for this business is that you are too crazy to excite the sus-
picion of those whom you may have to watch. For the affair
may be a trick. If so, I hope and believe that Hickey has no
hand in it. Still, it is my duty to take every precaution.'

'Cardinal may I ask whether traces of insanity have ever
appeared in our family?'

'Except in you and my grandmother, no. She was a Pole;
and you resemble her personally. Why do you ask?'

'Because it has often occurred to me that you are, perhaps,
a little cracked. Excuse my candour, but a man who has devot-

ed his life to the pursuit of a red hat, who accuses everyone else besides himself of being mad, and who is disposed to listen seriously to a tale of a peripatetic graveyard, can hardly be quite sane. Depend upon it, Uncle, you want rest and change. The blood of your Polish grandmother is in your veins.'

'I hope I may not be committing a sin in sending a ribald on the Church's affairs,' he replied, fervently. 'However, we must use the instruments put into our hands. Is it agreed that you go?'

'Had you not delayed me with this story, which I might as well have learned on the spot, I should have been there already.'

'There is no occasion for impatience, Zeno. I must first send to Hickey to find a place for you. I shall tell him that you are going to recover your health, as, in fact, you are. And, Zeno, in heaven's name be discreet. Try to act like a man of sense. Do not dispute with Hickey on matters of religion. Since you are my nephew, you had better not disgrace me.'

'I shall become an ardent Catholic, and do you infinite credit, Uncle.'

'I wish you would, although you would hardly be an acquisition to the Church. And now I must turn you out. It is nearly three o'clock, and I need some sleep. Do you know your way back to your hotel?'

'I need not stir. I can sleep in this chair. Go to bed and never mind me.'

'I shall not close my eyes until you are safely out of the house. Come, rouse yourself and say good night.'

The following is a copy of my first report to the cardinal:

> Four Mile Water,
> County Wicklow,
> 10 August

My Dear Uncle,

The miracle is genuine. I have affected perfect credulity in order to throw the Hickeys and the countryfolk off their guard with me. I have listened to their method of convincing sceptical strangers. I have examined the ordnance maps, and cross-examined the neighbouring Protestant gentlefolk. I have spent a day upon the ground on each side of the water, and have visited it at midnight. I have considered the upheaval theories, subsidence theories, volcanic theories, and tidal wave theories which the provincial *savants* have suggested. They are all untenable. There is only one scoffer in the district, an Orangeman; and he admits the removal of the cemetery, but says it was dug and transplanted in the night by a body of men under the command of Fr Tom. This also is out of the question. The interment of Brimstone Billy was the first which had taken place for four years; and his is the only grave which bears a trace of recent digging. It is alone on the north bank, and the inhabitants shun it after nightfall. As each passer-by during the day throws a stone upon it, it will soon be marked by a large cairn. The grave-yard, with a ruined stone chapel still standing in its midst, is on the south side. You may send down a committee to investigate the matter as soon as you please. There can be no doubt as to the miracle having actually taken place, as recorded by Hickey. As for me, I have grown so accustomed to it that if the County Wicklow were to waltz off with me to Middlesex, I should be quite impatient of any expressions of surprise from my friends in London.

Is not the above a businesslike statement? Away, then, with this stale miracle. If you would see for yourself a miracle which can never pall, a vision of youth and health to be crowned with garlands for ever, come down and see Kate Hickey, whom you suppose to be a little girl. Illusion, my Lord Cardinal, illusion! She is seventeen, with a bloom and a brogue that would lay your asceticism in ashes at a flash. To her I am an object of wonder, a strange man bred in wicked cities. She is courted by six feet of farming material, chopped off a spare length of coarse humanity by the Almighty, and flung into Wicklow to plough the fields. His name is Phil Langan; and he hates me. I have to consort with him for the sake of Fr Tom, whom I entertain vastly by stories of your wild oats sown at Salamanca. I exhausted all my authentic anecdotes the first day; and now I invent gallant escapades with Spanish donnas, in which you figure as a youth of unstable morals. This delights Fr Tom infinitely. I feel that I have done you a service by thus casting on the cold sacerdotal abstraction which formerly represented you in Kate's imagination a ray of vivifying passion.

What a county this is! A Hesperidean garden: such skies! Adieu, Uncle.

Zeno Legge

Behold me, then, at Four Mile Water, in love. I had been in love frequently; but not oftener than once a year had I encountered a woman who affected me as seriously as Kate Hickey. She was so shrewd, and yet so flippant! When I spoke of art she yawned. When I deplored the sordidness of the world she laughed and called me 'poor fellow'! When I told her what a treasure of beauty and freshness she had she ridiculed me. When I reproached her with her brutality she became angry and sneered at me for being what she called a fine gentleman. One sunny afternoon we were standing at the gate of her uncle's house, she looking down the dusty road for the detestable Langan, I watching the spotless azure sky, when she said:

'How soon are you going back to London?'

'I am not going back to London, Miss Hickey. I am not yet tired of Four Mile Water.'

'I'm sure Four Mile Water ought to be proud of your approbation.'

'You disapprove of my liking it, then? Or is it that you grudge me the happiness I have found here? I think Irish ladies grudge a man a moment's peace.'

'I wonder you have ever prevailed on yourself to associate with Irish ladies, since they are so far beneath you.'

'Did I say they were beneath me, Miss Hickey? I feel that I have made a deep impression on you.'

'Indeed! Yes, you're quite right. I assure you I can't sleep at night for thinking of you, Mr Legge. It's the best a Christian can do, seeing you think so mighty little of yourself.'

'You are triply wrong, Miss Hickey: wrong to be sarcastic with me, wrong to pretend that there is anything unreasonable in my belief that you think of me sometimes, and wrong to discourage the candour with which I always avow that I think constantly of myself.'

'Then you had better not speak to me, since I have no manners.'

'Again! Did I say you had no manners? The warmest expressions of regard from my mouth seem to reach your ears transformed into insults. Were I to repeat the Litany of the Blessed Virgin, you would retort as though I had been reproaching you. This is because you hate me. You never misunderstand Langan, whom you love.'

'I don't know what London manners are, Mr Legge; but in Ireland gentlemen are expected to mind their own business. How dare you say I love Mr Langan?'

'Then you do not love him?'

'It is nothing to you whether I love him or not.'

'Nothing to me that you hate me and love another?'

'I did not say that I hated you. You are not so very clever yourself at understanding what people say, though you make such a fuss because they don't understand you.' Here, as she glanced down the road again, she suddenly looked glad.

'Aha!' I said.

'What do you mean by "Aha"?'

'No matter. I will now show you what a man's sympathy is. As you perceived just then, Langan – who is too tall for his age, by-the-by – is coming to pay you a visit. Well, instead of staying with you, as a jealous woman would, I will withdraw.'

'I don't care whether you go or stay, I'm sure. I wonder what you would give to be as fine a man as Mr Langan.'

'All I possess: I swear it! But solely because you admire tall men more than broad views. Mr Langan may be defined geometrically as length without breadth; altitude without position; a line on the landscape, not a point in it.'

'How very clever you are!'

'You do not understand me, I see. Here comes your lover, stepping over the wall like a camel. And here go I, out through the gate like a Christian. Good afternoon, Mr Langan. I am going because Miss Hickey has something to say to you about me which she would rather not say in my presence. You will excuse me?'

'Oh, I'll excuse you,' said he boorishly. I smiled, and went out. Before I was quite out of hearing, Kate whispered vehemently to him, 'I hate that fellow.'

I smiled again; but I had scarcely done so when my spirits fell. I walked hastily away with a coarse threatening sound in my ears like that of the clarinets whose sustained low notes darken the woodland in 'Der Freischutz'. I found myself presently at the graveyard. It was a barren place, enclosed by a mud wall with a gate to admit funerals, and numerous gaps to admit the peasantry, who made short cuts across it as they went to and fro between Four Mile Water and the market town. The graves were mounds overgrown with grass: there was no keeper; nor were there flowers, railings or any of the conventionalities that make an English graveyard repulsive. A great thorn-bush, near what was called the grave of the holy sisters, was covered with scraps of cloth and flannel, attached by peasant women who had prayed before it. There were three kneeling there as I entered, for the reputation of the place had been revived of late by the miracle, and a ferry had been established close by, to conduct visitors over the route taken by the graveyard. From where I stood I could see on the opposite bank the heap of stones, perceptibly increased since my last visit, marking the deserted grave of Brimstone Billy. I strained my eyes broodingly at it for some minutes, and then descended the riverbank and entered the boat.

'Good evenin' t' your honour,' said the ferryman, and set to work to draw the boat hand-over-hand by a rope stretched across the water.

'Good evening. Is your business beginning to fall off yet?'

'Faith, it never was as good as it might ha' been. The people that comes from the south side can see Billy's grave – Lord have mercy on him – across the wather; and they think bad of payin' a penny to put a stone over him. Your honour is the third I've brought from south to north this blessed day.'

'When do most people come? In the afternoon, I suppose?'

'All hours, sur, except afther dusk. There isn't a sowl in the counthry ud come within sight of that grave wanst the sun goes down.'

'And you! Do you stay here all night by yourself?'

'The holy heavens forbid! Is it me stay here all night? No, your honour; I tether the boat at siven o'hlyock, and lave Brimstone Billy – God forgimme! – to take care of it till mornin'.'

'It will be stolen some night, I'm afraid.'

'Arra, who'd dar come next or near it, let alone stale it? Faith, I'd think twice before lookin' at it meself in the dark. God bless your honour, and gran'che long life.'

I had given him sixpence. I went to the reprobate's grave

and stood at the foot of it, looking at the sky, gorgeous with the descent of the sun. To my English eyes, accustomed to giant trees, broad lawns, and stately mansions, the landscape was wild and inhospitable. The ferryman was already tugging at the rope on his way back (I had told him I did not intend to return that way), and presently I saw him make the painter fast to the south bank; put on his coat; and trudge homeward. I turned towards the grave at my feet. Those who had interred Brimstone Billy, working hastily at an unlawful hour, and in fear of molestation by the people, had hardly dug a grave. They had scooped out earth enough to hide their burden, and no more. A stray goat had kicked away a corner of the mound and exposed the coffin. It occurred to me, as I took some of the stones from the cairn, and heaped them so as to repair the breach, that had the miracle been the work of a body of men, they would have moved the one grave instead of the many. Even from a supernatural point of view, it seemed strange that the sinner should have banished the elect, when, by their superior numbers, they might so much more easily have banished him.

It was almost dark when I left the spot. After a walk of half a mile, I recrossed the water by a bridge, and returned to the farmhouse in which I lodged. Here, finding that I had had enough of solitude, I only stayed to take a cup of tea. Then I went to Fr Hickey's cottage.

Kate was alone when I entered. She looked up quickly as I opened the door, and turned away disappointed when she recognised me.

'Be generous for once,' I said. 'I have walked about aimlessly for hours in order to avoid spoiling the beautiful afternoon for you by my presence. When the sun was up I withdrew my shadow from your path. Now that darkness has fallen, shed some light on mine. May I stay half an hour?'

'You may stay as long as you like, of course. My uncle will soon be home. He is clever enough to talk to you.'

'What! More sarcasms! Come, Miss Hickey, help me to spend a pleasant evening. It will only cost you a smile. I am somewhat cast down. Four Mile Water is a paradise; but without you, it would be a little lonely.'

'It must be very lonely for you. I wonder why you came here.'

'Because I heard that the women here were all Zerlinas, like you, and the men Masettos, like Mr Phil – where are you going to?'

'Let me pass, Mr Legge. I had intended never speaking to you again after the way you went on about Mr Langan today; and I wouldn't either, only my uncle made me promise not to take any notice of you, because you were – no matter; but I won't listen to you any more on the subject.'

'Do not go. I swear never to mention his name again. I beg your pardon for what I said: you shall have no further cause for complaint. Will you forgive me?'

She sat down, evidently disappointed by my submission. I took a chair, and placed myself near her. She tapped the floor impatiently with her foot. I saw that there was not a movement I could make, not a look, not a tone of my voice, which did not irritate her.

'You were remarking,' I said, 'that your uncle desired you to take no notice of me because – '

She closed her lips, and did not answer.

'I fear I have offended you again by my curiosity. But indeed, I had no idea that he had forbidden you to tell me the reason.'

'He did not forbid me. Since you are so determined to find out – '

'No, excuse me. I do not wish to know, I am sorry I asked.'

'Indeed! Perhaps you would be sorrier still to be told. I only made a secret of it out of consideration for you.'

'Then your uncle has spoken ill of me behind my back. If that be so, there is no such thing as a true man in Ireland. I would not have believed it on the word of any woman alive save yourself.'

'I never said my uncle was a backbiter. Just to show you what he thinks of you, I will tell you, whether you want to know it or not, that he bid me not mind you because you were only a poor mad creature, sent down here by your family to be out of harm's way.'

'Oh, Miss Hickey!'

'There now! You have got it out of me; and I wish I had bit my tongue out first. I sometimes think – that I mayn't sin! – that you have a bad angel in you.'

'I am glad you told me this,' I said gently. 'Do not reproach yourself for having done so, I beg. Your uncle has been misled by what he has heard of my family, who are all more or less insane. Far from being mad, I am actually the only rational man named Legge in the three kingdoms. I will prove this to you, and at the same time keep your indiscretion in countenance, by telling you something I ought not to tell you. It is this. I am not here as an invalid or a chance tourist. I am here to investigate the miracle. The cardinal, a shrewd if somewhat erratic man, selected mine from all the long heads at his disposal to come down here, and find out the truth of Fr Hickey's story. Would he have entrusted such a task to a madman, think you?'

'The truth of – who dared to doubt my uncle's word? And so you are a spy, a dirty informer.'

I started. The adjective she had used, though probably the commonest expression of contempt in Ireland, is revolting to an Englishman.

'Miss Hickey,' I said, 'there is in me, as you have said, a bad angel. Do not shock my good angel – who is a person of taste – quite away from my heart, lest the other be left undisputed monarch of it. Hark! The chapel bell is ringing. Can you, with that sound softening the darkness of the village night, cherish a feeling of spite against one who admires you?'

'You come between me and my prayers,' she said hysterically, and began to sob. She had scarcely done so, when I heard voices without. Then Langan and the priest entered.

'Oh, Phil,' she cried, running to him, 'take me away from him: I can't bear – ' I turned towards him, and showed him my dog-tooth in a false smile. He felled me at one stroke, as he might have felled a poplar tree.

'Murdher!' exclaimed the priest. 'What are you doin', Phil?'

'He's an informer,' sobbed Kate. 'He came down here to spy on you, Uncle, and to try and show that the blessed miracle was a make-up. I knew it long before he told me, by his insulting ways. He wanted to make love to me.'

I rose with difficulty from beneath the table, where I had lain motionless for a moment.

'Sir,' I said, 'I am somewhat dazed by the recent action of Mr Langan, whom I beg, the next time he converts himself into a fulling-mill, to do so at the expense of a man more nearly his equal in strength than I. What your niece has told you is partly true. I am indeed the cardinal's spy; and I have already reported to him that the miracle is a genuine one. A committee of gentlemen will wait on you tomorrow to verify it, at my suggestion. I have thought that the proof might be regarded by them as more complete if you were taken by surprise. Miss Hickey, that I admire all that is admirable in you is but to say that I have a sense of the beautiful. To say that I love you would be mere profanity. Mr Langan, I have in my pocket a loaded pistol, which I carry from a silly English prejudice against your countrymen. Had I been the Hercules of the plough-tail, and you in my place, I should have been a dead man now. Do not redden; you are safe as far as I am concerned.'

'Let me tell you before you leave my house for good,' said Fr Hickey, who seemed to have become unreasonably angry, 'that you should never have crossed my threshold if I had known you were a spy; no, not if your uncle were his Holiness the Pope himself.'

Here a frightful thing happened to me. I felt giddy, and put my hand to my head. Three warm drops trickled over it. Instantly I became murderous. My mouth filled with blood, my eyes were blinded with it; I seemed to drown in it. My hand went involuntarily to the pistol. It is my habit to obey my impulses instantaneously. Fortunately, the impulse to kill vanished before a sudden perception of how I might miraculously humble the mad vanity which these foolish people had turned up in me. The blood receded from my ears; and I again heard and saw distinctly.

'And let *me* tell you,' Langan was saying, 'that if you think yourself handier with cold lead than you are with your fists, I'll exchange shots with you, and welcome, whenever you please. Fr Tom's credit is the same to me as my own, and if you say a word against it, you lie.'

'His credit is in my hands,' I said. 'I am the cardinal's witness. Do you defy me?'

'There is the door,' said the priest, holding it open before me. 'Until you can undo the visible work of God's hand your testimony can do no harm to me.'

'Fr Hickey,' I replied, 'before the sun rises again upon Four Mile Water, I will undo the visible work of God's hand, and bring the pointing finger of the scoffer upon your altar.'

I bowed to Kate, and walked out. It was so dark that I could not at first see the garden-gate. Before I found it, I heard through the window Fr Hickey's voice, saying, 'I wouldn't for ten pound that this had happened, Phil. He's as mad as a March hare. The cardinal told me so.'

I returned to my lodging, and took a cold bath to cleanse the blood from my neck and shoulder. The effect of the blow I had received was so severe, that even after the bath and a light meal I felt giddy and languid. There was an alarum-clock on the mantelpiece. I wound it; set the alarum for half past twelve; muffled it so that it should not disturb the people in the adjoining room; and went to bed, where I slept soundly for an hour and a quarter. Then the alarum roused me, and I sprang up before I was thoroughly awake. Had I hesitated, the desire to relapse into perfect sleep would have overpowered me. Although the muscles of my neck were painfully stiff, and my hands unsteady from my nervous disturbance, produced by the interruption of my first slumber, I dressed myself resolutely and, after taking a draught of cold water, stole out of the house. It was exceedingly dark and I had some difficulty in finding the cow-house, whence I borrowed a spade, and a truck with wheels, ordinarily used for moving sacks of potatoes. These I carried in my hands until I was beyond earshot of the house, when I put the spade on the truck, and wheeled it along the road to the cemetery. When I approached the water, knowing that no one would dare to come thereabout at such an hour, I made greater haste, no longer concerning myself about the rattling of the wheels. Looking across to the opposite bank, I could see a phosphorescent glow, marking the lonely grave of Brimstone Billy. This helped me to find the ferry station, where, after wandering a little and stumbling often, I found the boat, and embarked with my implements. Guided by the rope, I crossed the water without difficulty; landed; made fast the boat; dragged the truck up the bank; and sat down to rest on the cairn at the grave. For nearly a quarter of an hour I sat watching the patches of jack-o'-lantern fire, and collecting my strength for the work before me. Then the distant bell of the chapel clock tolled one. I rose, took the spade, and in about ten minutes uncovered the coffin, which smelt horribly. Keeping to windward of it, and using the spade as a lever, I contrived with great labour to place it on the truck. I wheeled it without accident to the landing-place, where, by placing the shafts of the truck upon the stern of the boat and lifting the foot by main strength, I succeeded in embarking my load after twenty minutes' toil, during which I got covered with clay and perspiration, and several times all but upset the boat. At the southern bank I had less difficulty in getting truck and coffin ashore, and dragging them up the graveyard.

It was now past two o'clock, and the dawn had begun, so that I had no further trouble from want of light. I wheeled the coffin to a patch of loamy soil which I had noticed in the afternoon near the grave of the holy sisters. I had warmed to my work; my neck no longer pained me; and I began to dig vigorously, soon making a shallow trench, deep enough to hide the coffin with the addition of a mound. The chill pearl-coloured morning had by this time quite dissipated the darkness. I could see, and was myself visible, for miles around. This alarmed me, and made me impatient to finish my task. Nevertheless, I was forced to rest for a moment before placing the coffin in the trench. I wiped my brow and wrists, and again looked about me. The tomb of the holy women, a massive slab supported on four stone spheres, was grey and wet with dew. Near it was the thorn-bush covered with rags, the newest of which were growing gaudy in the radiance which was stretching up from the coast on the east. It was time to finish my work. I seized the truck; laid it alongside the grave; and gradually prised the coffin off with the spade until it rolled over into the trench with a hollow sound like a drunken remonstrance from the sleeper within. I shovelled the earth round and over it, working as fast as possible. In less than a quarter of an hour it was buried. Ten minutes more sufficed to make the mound symmetrical, and to clear the traces of my work from the adjacent sward. Then I flung down the spade; threw up my arms; and vented a sign of relief and triumph. But I recoiled as I saw that I was standing on a barren common, covered with furze. No product of man's handiwork was near me except my truck and spade and the grave of Brimstone Billy, now as lonely as before. I turned towards the water. On the opposite bank was the cemetery, with the tomb of the holy women, the thorn-bush with its rags stirring in the morning breeze, and the broken mud wall. The ruined chapel was there too, not a stone shaken from its crumbling walls, not a sign to show that it and its precinct were less rooted in their place than the eternal hills around.

I looked down at the grave with a pang of compassion for the unfortunate Wolfe Tone Fitzgerald, with whom the blessed would not rest. I was even astonished, though I had worked expressly to this end. But the birds were astir, and the cocks crowing. My landlord was an early riser. I put the spade on the truck again, and hastened back to the farm, where I replaced them in the cow-house. Then I stole into the house, and took a clean pair of boots, an overcoat, and a silk hat. These, with a change of linen, were sufficient to make my appearance respectable. I went out again, bathed in the Four Mile Water, took a last look at the cemetery, and walked to Wicklow, whence I travelled by the first train to Dublin.

Some months later, at Cairo, I received a packet of Irish newspapers and a leading article, cut from the *Times*, on the subject of the miracle. Fr Hickey had suffered the meed of his inhospitable conduct. The committee, arriving at Four Mile Water the day after I left, had found the graveyard exactly where it had formerly stood. Fr Hickey, taken by surprise, had attempted to defend himself by a confused statement, which led the committee to declare finally that the miracle was a gross imposture. The *Times*, commenting on this after adducing a number of examples of priestly craft, remarked:

We are glad to learn that the Rev. Mr Hickey has been permanently relieved of his duties as the parish priest of Four Mile Water by his ecclesiastical superior. It is less gratifying to have to record that it has been found possible to obtain two hundred signatures to a memorial embodying the absurd defence offered to the committee, and expressing unabated confidence in the integrity of Mr Hickey.

A VERY MERRY CHRISTMAS

by Morley Callaghan

AFTER MIDNIGHT ON CHRISTMAS Eve hundreds of people prayed at the crib of the Infant Jesus which was to the right of the altar under the evergreen-tree branches in St Malachi's Church. That night there had been a heavy fall of wet snow, and there was a muddy path up to the crib. Both Sylvanus O'Meara, the old caretaker who had helped prepare the crib, and Fr Gorman, the stout, red-faced, excitable parish priest, had agreed it was the most lifelike tableau of the Child Jesus in a corner of the stable at Bethlehem they had ever had in the church.

But early on Christmas morning Fr Gorman came running to see O'Meara, the blood all drained out of his face and his hands pumping up and down at the sides as he shouted, 'A terrible thing has happened. Where is the Infant Jesus? The crib's empty.'

O'Meara, who was a devout, innocent, wondering old man, who prayed a lot and always felt very close to God in the church, was bewildered and he whispered, 'Who could have taken it? Taken it where?'

'Take a look in the crib yourself, man, if you don't believe me,' the priest said, and he grabbed the caretaker by the arm, marched him into the church and over to the crib and showed him that the figure of the Infant Jesus was gone.

'Someone took it, of course. It didn't fly away. But who took it, that's the question?' the priest said. 'When was the last time you saw it?'

'I know it was here last night,' O'Meara said, 'because after the midnight Mass when everybody else had gone home I saw Mrs Farrell and her little boy kneeling up here, and when they stood up I wished them a merry Christmas. You don't think she'd touch it, do you?'

'What nonsense, O'Meara. There's not a finer woman in the parish. I'm going over to her house for dinner today.'

'I noticed that she wanted to go home, but the little boy wanted to stay here and keep praying by the crib; but after they went home I said a few prayers myself and the Infant Jesus was still there.'

Grabbing O'Meara by the arm the priest whispered excitedly, 'It must be the work of communists or atheists.' There was a sudden rush of blood to his face. 'This isn't the first time they've struck at us,' he said.

'What would communists want with a figure of the Infant Jesus?' O'Meara asked innocently. 'They wouldn't want to have it to be reminded that God was with them. I didn't think they could bear to have Him with them.'

'They'd take it to mock us, of course, and to desecrate the church. O'Meara, you don't seem to know much about the times we live in. Why did they set fire to the church?'

O'Meara said nothing because he was very loyal and didn't like to remind the priest that the little fire they had in the church a few months ago was caused by a cigarette butt the priest had left in his pocket when he was changing into his vestments, so he was puzzled and silent for a while and then whispered, 'Maybe someone really wanted to take God away, do you think so?'

'Take Him out of the church?'

'Yes. Take Him away.'

'How could you take God out of the church, man? Don't be stupid.'

'But maybe someone thought you could, don't you see?'

'O'Meara, you talk like an old idiot. Don't you realise you play right into the hands of the atheists, saying such things? Do we believe in an image of God? Do we worship idols? We do not. No more of that, then. If communists and atheists tried to burn this church once, they'll not stop till they desecrate it. God help us, why is my church marked out for this?' He got terribly excited and rushed away shouting, 'I'm going to phone the police.'

It looked like the beginning of a terrible Christmas Day for the parish. The police came, and were puzzled, and talked to everybody. Newspapermen came. They took pictures of the church and of Fr Gorman, who had just preached a sermon that startled the congregation because he grew very eloquent on the subject of vandal outrages to the house of God. Men and women stood outside the church in their best clothes and talked very gravely. Everybody wanted to know what the thief would do with the image of the Infant Jesus. They all were wounded, stirred and wondering. There certainly was going to be something worth talking about at a great many Christmas dinners in the neighbourhood.

But Sylvanus O'Meara went off by himself and was very sad. From time to time he went into the church and looked at the empty crib. He had all kinds of strange thoughts. He told himself that if someone really wanted to hurt God, then wishing harm to Him really hurt Him, for what other way was there of hurting Him? Last night he had had the feeling that God was all around the crib, and now it felt as if God wasn't there at all. It wasn't just that the image of the Infant Jesus was gone, but someone had done violence to that spot and had driven God away from it. He told himself that things could be done that would make God want to leave a place. It was very hard to know where God was. Of course, he would always be in the church, but where had that part of Him that had seemed to be all around the crib gone?

It wasn't a question that he could ask the little groups of astounded parishioners who stood on the footpath outside the church, because they felt like wagging their fingers and puffing their cheeks out and talking about what was happening to God in Mexico and Spain.

But when they had all gone home to eat their Christmas dinners, O'Meara, himself, began to feel a little hungry. He went out and stood in front of the church and was feeling thankful that there was so much snow for the children on Christmas Day when he saw that splendid and prominent woman, Mrs Farrell, coming along the street with her little boy. On Mrs Farrell's face there was a grim and desperate expression and she was taking such long fierce strides that the five-year-old boy, whose hand she held so tightly, could hardly keep up with her and pull his big red sleigh. Sometimes the little boy tried to lean back and was a dead weight and then she pulled his feet off the ground while he whimpered, 'Oh, gee, oh, gee, let me go.' His red snowsuit was all covered with snow as if he had been rolling on the road.

'Merry Christmas, Mrs Farrell,' O'Meara said. And he called to the boy. 'Not happy on Christmas Day? What's the matter, son?'

'Merry Christmas, indeed, Mr O'Meara,' the woman snapped at him. She was not accustomed to paying much attention to the caretaker. A curt nod was all she ever gave him, and now she was furiously angry and too mortified to bother with him. 'Where's Fr Gorman?' she demanded.

'Still at the police station, I think.'

'At the police station! God help us, did you hear that, Jimmie?' she said, and she gave such a sharp tug at the boy's arm that she spun him around in the snow behind her skirts where he cowered, watching O'Meara with a curiously steady pair of fine blue eyes. He wiped away a mat of hair from his forehead as he watched and waited. 'Oh, Lord, this is terrible,' Mrs Farrell said. 'What will I do?'

'What's the matter, Mrs Farrell?'

'I didn't do anything,' the child said. 'I was coming back here. Honest I was, Mister.'

'Mr O'Meara,' the woman began, as if coming down from a great height to the level of an unimportant and simple-minded old man, 'maybe you could do something for us. Look on the sleigh.'

O'Meara saw an old coat was wrapped around something on the sleigh, and stooping to lift it, he saw the figure of the Infant Jesus there. He was so delighted he only looked up at Mrs Farrell and shook his head in wonder and said, 'It's back and nobody harmed it at all.'

'I'm ashamed, I'm terribly ashamed, Mr O'Meara. You don't know how mortified I am,' she said, 'but the child really didn't know what he was doing. It's a disgrace to us, I know. It's my fault that I haven't trained him better, though God knows I've tried to drum respect for the church into him.' She gave such a jerk at the child's hand that he slid on his knee in the snow, keeping his eyes on O'Meara.

Still unbelieving, O'Meara asked, 'You mean he really took it from the church?'

'He did, he really did.'

'Fancy that. Why, child, that was a terrible thing to do,' O'Meara said. 'Whatever got into you?' Completely mystified, he turned to Mrs Farrell, but he was so relieved to have the figure of the Infant Jesus back without there having been any great scandal that he couldn't help putting his hand gently on the child's head.

'It's all right, and you don't need to say anything,' the child said, pulling away angrily from his mother, and yet he never took his eyes off O'Meara, as if he felt there was some bond between them. Then he looked down at his mits, fumbled with them and looked up steadily and said, 'It's all right, isn't it, Mister?'

'It was early this morning, right after he got up, almost the first thing he must have done on Christmas Day,' Mrs Farrell said. 'He must have walked right in and picked it up and taken it out to the street.'

'But what got into him?'

'He makes no sense about it. He says he had to do it.'

'And so I did, 'cause it was a promise,' the child said. 'I promised last night, I promised God that if He would make Mother bring me a big red sleigh for Christmas I would give Him the first ride on it.'

'Don't think I've taught the child foolish things,' Mrs Farrell said. 'I'm sure he meant no harm. He didn't understand at all what he was doing.'

'Yes I did,' the child said stubbornly.

'Shut up, child,' she said, shaking him.

O'Meara knelt down till his eyes were on a level with the child's and they looked at each other till they felt close together and he said, 'But why did you want to do that for God?'

"Cause it's a swell sleigh, and I thought God would like it.'

Mrs Farrell, fussing and red-faced, said, 'Don't you worry. I'll see he's punished by having the sleigh taken away from him.'

But O'Meara, who had picked up the figure of the Infant Jesus, was staring down at the red sleigh; and suddenly he had a feeling of great joy, of the illumination of strange good tidings, a feeling that this might be the most marvellous Christmas Day in the whole history of the city, for God must surely have been with the child, with him on a joyous, carefree holiday sleigh ride, as he ran along those streets and pulled the sleigh. And O'Meara turned to Mrs Farrell, his face bright with joy, and said, commandingly, with a look in his eyes that awed her, 'Don't you dare say a word to him, and don't you dare touch that sleigh, do you hear? I think God did like it.'

160

Acknowledgements

Thanks are due to the following for permission to reprint the material indicated: The Devin-Adair Company for 'All the Sweet Buttermilk...' by Donagh MacDonagh from *44 Irish Short Stories*, edited by Devin Garrity, copyright © 1955 by Devin-Adair Company; John Farquharson Ltd for 'Trinket's Colt' from *Some Experiences of an Irish RM* by E.O. Somerville and Martin Ross; Eamon Kelly for 'A Matter of Opinion', 'The Looking Glass' and 'The Umbrella'; *Dublin Opinion* for 'Way of Women' by Paul Jones; The Hutchinson Publishing Group Ltd for 'Ireland's Different to England – See?' from *Brewing Up in the Basement* by Patrick Campbell, copyright © Patrick Campbell 1963; Lady Dunsany for 'Little Tim Brannehan' by Lord Dunsany; Cyril Daly and *The Sign* for 'Homeward' by Cyril Daly, reprinted from *The Sign*, National Catholic Magazine, Union City, New Jersey, January 1967 issue; Alfred A. Knopf for 'Peasants' from *The Stories of Frank O'Connor*, copyright © 1936 by Frank O'Connor; Atlantic-Little, Brown and Company for 'Two of a Kind' from *I Remember, I Remember* by Seán O'Faolain, copyright © 1959, 1961 by Seán O'Faolain; A.P. Watt & Son, Collins-Knowlton-Wing, Inc. and the Estate of Leslie A. Montgomery for 'A Persian Tale' from *Lobster Salad* by Lynn Doyle, copyright © 1922 by Leslie A. Montgomery and Alan A. Montgomery; Doubleday & Company Inc. for 'Bird Milligan' from *A Weekend in the Middle of the West* by Oliver St John Gogarty, copyright © 1958 by Oliver D. Gogarty, Executor of the Estate of Oliver St John Gogarty; Harold Matson Company, Inc. for 'A Very Merry Christmas' by Morley Callaghan, copyright © 1937, 1965 by Morley Callaghan.